William R. Warner

Physicians´ formulary of reliable and permanent soluble coated pills parvules etc.

William R. Warner

Physicians´ formulary of reliable and permanent soluble coated pills parvules etc.

ISBN/EAN: 9783742818928

Manufactured in Europe, USA, Canada, Australia, Japa

Cover: Foto ©Andreas Hilbeck / pixelio.de

Manufactured and distributed by brebook publishing software
(www.brebook.com)

William R. Warner

Physicians´ formulary of reliable and permanent soluble coated pills parvules etc.

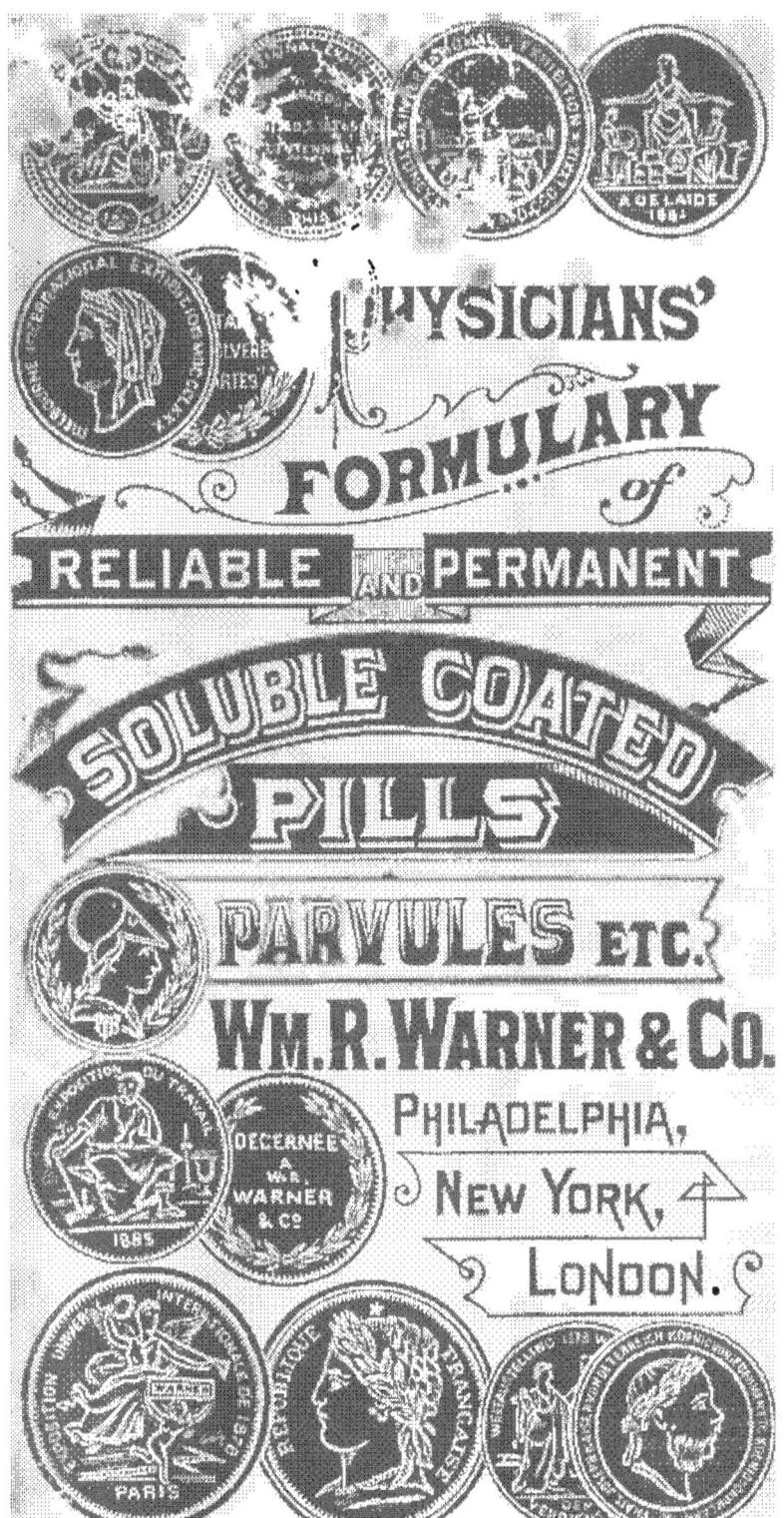

PHYSICIANS' FORMULARY of

RELIABLE AND PERMANENT

SOLUBLE COATED PILLS

PARVULES ETC.

WM. R. WARNER & CO.

PHILADELPHIA,
NEW YORK,
LONDON.

FOR THE SPEEDY RELIEF OF

Nervous Headache and Brain Fatigue.

BROMO

(WARNER & CO.)

SODA

Useful in Nervous Headache, Sleeplessness, Excessive Study, Over Brainwork, Sea Sickness, Epilepsy, Nervous Debility, Mania, etc., etc.

DOSE.—A heaping teaspoonful in half a glass of water, to be repeated after an interval of thirty minutes, if necessary.

It is claimed by some prominent specialists in nervous diseases, that the Sodium Salt is more acceptable to the stomach than the Bromide Potassium. An almost certain relief is given by the administration of this Effervescing Salt. It is also used with advantage in INDIGESTION, DEPRESSION following alcoholic and other excesses, as well as NERVOUS HEADACHE. It affords speedy relief for MENTAL and PHYSICAL EXHAUSTION.

PREPARED ONLY BY

WM. R. WARNER & CO.

MANUFACTURERS OF

SOLUBLE COATED PILLS,

PHILADELPHIA and NEW YORK.

PHYSICIANS'

COMPLETE

FORMULA BOOK

GIVING DOSES AND MEDICAL PROPERTIES

—OF—

WM. R. WARNER & CO.'S

RELIABLE SOLUBLE-COATED

PILLS,

GRANULES and PARVULES

WITH REFERENCE NOTES RESPECTING

POISONS AND ANTIDOTES, DISEASES AND REMEDIES, ETC., ETC., ETC.

PUBLISHED BY

WILLIAM R. WARNER & CO.

PHILADELPHIA AND NEW YORK.

1888.

CONTENTS.

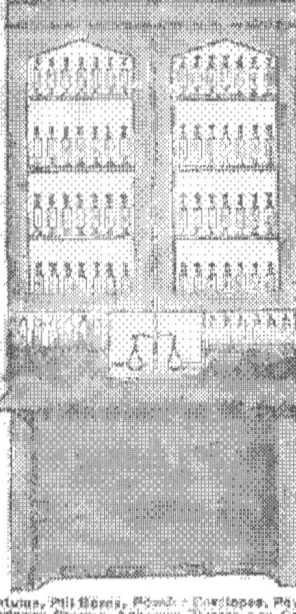

WARNER & CO.'S

Soluble Coated Pills.

These Pills are unsurpassed in their medicinal qualities, as only the best materials enter into their composition, while the most scrupulous care is exercised in their manufacture.

An extended laboratory experience comprising unceasing attention to details during a period of more than a quarter of a century enables us to arrive at results otherwise unattainable.

We claim a method of coating which remains permanent and avoids the necessity for drying the mass so hard as to render it insoluble or inert. This scientific method which we do not hesitate to call our own is fully recognized and appreciated, as is demonstrated by the confidence reposed and the success attained.

It is our wish to emphatically impress upon the minds of prescribers, that our make of Pills will produce the effects as should be expected in connection with the drug employed, and that every other desire is subordinate to this end. We thank the Profession for the very liberal endorsement and patronage that has been accorded us and offer our assurance that our efforts shall, as heretofore, be directed towards the production of the highest class of Pharmaceutical preparations.

Respectfully,

WM. R. WARNER & CO.

TO THE MEDICAL PROFESSION.

While presenting this revised edition of our Formulary we take the opportunity to extend our thanks to our many friends; who have aided us by their patronage and influence in distributing Pharmaceutical Preparations of the highest standard and to express the hope that our efforts, in this direction, may continue to gain for us a confidence and feeling that our experience covering as it has, a period of thirty years and comprising deep scientific research and skilful manipulations, in conjunction with a conscientious desire to produce only the best, should at least warrant us in claiming a perfection of manufacture unexcelled.

Such facts are worthy the attention of Practitioners who are called upon to battle with disease, and who must in using ready prepared medicines, depend upon the correctness of manufacture to gain the looked for therepeutical effects, whereby their own reputations are sustained and the ills of their patients alleviated

It may be well, in this connection, to reiterate that our endeavors have always been directed towards the production of first-class preparations, regardless of cost and passing the question of extreme cheapness which so often arises through competition and an anxiety to dispose of products; all of which very naturally has a tendency to depreciate quality correspondingly with the falling off in price.

We maintain that quality is of primary importance and in this we flatter ourselves that we have received the undivided encouragement and support of an intelligent profession, throughout the course of our business career.

With these few preliminary words outlining our policy, we beg leave to suggest the importance of specifying Warner & Co.'s make when ordering or prescribing.

Very Respectfully,

WM. R. WARNER & CO.

A COMPLETE FORMULA BOOK

—OF—

WM. R. WARNER & CO.'S

RELIABLE AND PERMANENT

SOLUBLE COATED

PILLS.

Of the United States Pharmacopœia and Recipes
of Eminent Physicians.

PILLS.	BOTTLE. 100	500
Abernethy's (Aperient)..............	75	3 50
Pulv. Aloes Socot., 2 grs.		
Pulv. Ipecac., 5–6 gr.		
Pil. Hydrarg., 1 gr.		
Ext. Hyoscyam., 2 grs.		
Acid Arsenious. 1-20, 1-30, 1-50 and 1-60 grs.......................	40	1 75
Medical properties—Anti-periodic, Alterative. Dose, 1 to 2.		
	75	3 50
Aconitia. 1-60 gr....................		
Med. prop.—Nerve Sedative. Dose, 1.*	75	3 50
Ague		
Med. prop.—Anti-periodic. Dose, 2 to 4.		
Chinoidin, 2 grs.		
Ext. Coloc. Comp. ⅓ gr.		
Ol. Pip. Nig., ⅛ gr.		
Ferri Sul., ½ gr.		
Aloes, U. S. P.......................	40	1 75
Med. prop.—Stimulating, Purgative. Dose, 1 to 3.		
Aloes Compound. (See Pil. Gentian Compound).....................	40	1 75
Med. prop.—Tonic, Purgative. Dose, 2 to 4.		
Aloes et Asafœtida, U. S. P.....	40	1 75
Med. prop.—Purgative, Anti-spasmodic. Dose, 2 to 5.		

PILLS.	BOTTLE.	
	100	500
Aloes et Ferri............... Med. prop.—Tonic, Purgative. Dose, 1 to 3. Pv. Aloes Socot., ½ gr. Pv. Zingiber Jam., 1 gr. Ferri Sul. Exs., 1 gr. Ext. Conii, ½ gr.	40	1 75
Aloes et Ferri, U. S. P. .... Med. prop.—Tonic, Purgative Dose, 1 to 3. Pur. Aloes, 1 gr. Aromat. Powd., 1 gr. Ferri Sul. Exs., 1 gr. Confect. Rose, q. s.	40	1 75
Aloes et Mastich. (Lady Webster). Med. prop.—Stimulating Purgative. Dose, 1 to 2.	50	2 25
Aloes et Myrrhæ, U. S. P...... Med. prop.—Cathartic, Emmenagogue. Dose, 3 to 6.	50	2 25
Aloes et Nue Vomicæ.......... Med. prop.—Tonic, Purgative. Dose, 1 to 2. Pulv. Aloes Soc., 1½ gr. Ext. Nuc. Vom., ½ gr.	50	2 25
Aloin. ½ gr........................ Med prop.—Laxative.	1 00	4 75
Aloin Comp....................... Med. prop.—Tonic, Laxative. Dose 1 to 2. Aloin, ⅛ gr. Ext. Belladou. ¼ gr. Podophyllin, ⅛ gr.	50	2 25
Aloin et Strychnin............... Med. prop.—Tonic, Laxative. Aloin, 1-5 gr. Strychnine, 1-60 gr.	60	2 75
Aloin et Strychnin. et Belladon......................... Used very largely and with great success in the treatment of habitual constipation. Med. prop.—Tonic, Laxative. Aloin, 1-5 gr. Strychnine, 1-60 gt. Ext. Belladon., ⅛ gr.	60	2 75

8

PILLS.	BOTTLE.	
	100	500
Aloin et Strychnin. et Bellad. Comp......................	75	3 50
Med. prop.		
Aloin, 1-5 gr.		
Ext. Belladon, ⅛ gr.		
Strychninæ, 1-60 gr.		
Ext. Cascara Sag., ½ gr.		
Alterative.....................	50	2 25
Med. prop.—Alterative, with tendency to Mercurial Impression. Dose, 1 to 2.		
Mass. Hydrarg., 1 gr.		
Pulv. Opii., ⅛ gr.		
Pulv. Ipecac., ⅛ gr.		
Alterative. (Dr. C. C. Cox).....	50	2 25
Med. prop.—Alterative, with tendency to Mercurial Impression. Dose, 1 to 2.		
Mass. Hydrarg., 1 gr.		
Pulv. Rhei., 1 gr.		
Sodii. Bicarb., 1 gr.		
Ammon. Bromid. 1 gr.........	75	3 50
Med. prop.—Sedative, Alterative, Re-solvent. Dose, 1.		
Analeptic....................	60	2 75
Med. prop.—Stimulant, Diaphoretic. Dose, 1 to 4.		
Pv. Antimonialis, ¾ gr.		
Pv. Res. Guaiac., 1 gr.		
Pv. Aloes Socot., ¾ gr.		
Pv. Myrrh., ½ gr.		
Anderson's Scot's.............	40	1 75
Med. prop.—Cathartic. 2 to 5.		
Pv. Aloes Socot.,		
Pv. Saponis,		
Pv. Colocynth.		
Pv. Gambogiæ.		
Anodyne.....................	75	3 50
Med. prop.—Anodyne. Dose, 2 to 5.		
Pv. Camphoræ, 1 gr.		
Morphin Acetas, 1-20 gr.		
Ext. Hyoscyami, 1 gr.		
Ol. Res. Capsici, 1-20 gr.		
Anthelmintic.................	1 00	4 75
Med. prop.—Anthelmintic. Dose, 1 to 2.		
Santonin, 1 gr.		
Calomel, 1 gr.		

PILLS.	BOTTLE.	
	100	500

Anti-Bilious (Vegetable)............ 50 | 2 25
Med. prop. — Cholagogue Cathartic.
   Dose, 2 to 3.
   Pv. Ext. Col. Co.,   2½ grs. }
   Podophyllin,   ¼ gr. }

Anti-Chill..................... 1 00 | 4 75
Med. prop.—Anti-periodic. Applicable
   to obstinate intermittents. Dose,
   1 to 2.
   Chinoidin,   1 gr. }
   Ferri Ferrocyanid,   1 gr. }
   Ol. Piper. Nig.,   1 gr. }
   Ac. Arsenious,   1-20 gr.}

Anti-Chlorotic.................. 75 | 3 50
Med. prop.—Anti-chlorotic. Dose 1 to 2
   Potass. Chlor.,   1 gr. }
   Ferri Chlor.,   ½ gr. }
   Pv. Podophylli.,   1 gr. }
   Pv. Myrrhæ,   ½ gr.}

Anti-Choromania............... 75 | 3 50
Med. prop.—Anti-spasmodic. Dose, 1
   to 2.
   Zinci Valer,   2 grs. }
   Ferri Valer,   ¼ gr. }
   Ext. Sumbul.,   ¼ gr. }

Anti-Constipation.............. 75 | 3 50
Dose, 1 to 4.
   Podophyllin,   1-10 gr.}
   Ext. Nuc. Vom.   ¼ gr. }
   Pv. Capsici,   ¼ gr. }
   Ext. Belladon.,   1-10 gr.}
   Ext. Hyoscyami,   ¼ gr. }

Anti-Constipation. (Palmer.)... 75 | 3 50
Dose, 1 to 2.
   Aloes Soc't   1 gr. }
   Ext. Hyoscyami,   1 gr. }
   Ext. Nuc Vom.,   ⅓ gr. }
   Ipecac Pulv.,   1-10 gr.}

Anti-Dyspeptic................. 1 00 | 4 75
Med prop.—Applicable where Debility
   and Impaired Digestion exist. Dose,
   1 to 2.
   Strychnine,   1-40 gr.}
   Ext. Belladon,   1-10 gr.}
   Pulv. Ipecac.,   1-10 gr.}
   Mass. Hydrarg.,   2 grs. }
   Ext. Coloc. Comp.   2 grs.}

PILLS.	BOTTLE.	
	100	500
Anti-Dyspeptic. (Fothergill).....	75	3 50
Dose, 1.		
Pv. Ipecac., ⅔ gr.		
Strychnine, 1–20 gr.		
Pv. Piper Nig. 1½ gr.		
Ext. Gentian, 1 gr.		
Anti-Malarial.....................	1 25	6 00
Med. prop.—Anti-malarial. Dose, 1 to 2		
Quininæ Sulph., 1 gr.		
Cinchoninæ Sulph., ⅛ gr.		
Ferri Sulph. Exs. ¼ gr.		
Ac. Arsenious, 1–40 gr.		
Anti-Malarial (Philadelphia).....	1 00	4 75
Med. prop.—Anti-malarial. Dose, 1 to 2.		
Ferri Sulph., 1 gr.		
Pv. Capsici, ⅛ gr.		
Cinchonid. Sulph., 2 grs.		
Strychnine, 1–30 gr.		
Anti-Malarial. (McCaw).........	1 50	7 25
Dose, 1 to 2.		
Quininæ Sulph., 1 gr.		
Ferri Sulph. Exs., ¼ gr.		
Ac. Arsenious, 1–30 gr.		
Gelsemin, ¼ gr.		
Podophyllin, ⅛ gr.		
Ol. Res. Pip. Nig., 1–10 gr.		
Antimonii Comp., U. S. P. (Pil. Plummer)......................	40	1 75
Med. prop.—Alterative. Dose, 1 to 3.		
Anti-Periodic.....................	80	3 75
Med. prop.—Anti-periodic. Dose 1 to 3.		
Cinchonidin Sulph., 1 gr.		
Res. Podophylli, 1–20 gr.		
Strychninæ Sul., 1–33 gr.		
Gelsemin, 1–20 gr.		
Ferri Sulph. Exs., ½ gr.		
Ol. Res. Capsici, 1–10 gtt.		
Anti-Periodic. (One-half size).....	45	2 00
Dose, 1 to 3.		
Anti-Spasmodic..................	75	3 50
Med. prop.—Anti-spasmodic. Dose, 1 to 2.		
Ext. Hyoscyami, ½ gr.		
Morphinæ Acetas., 1–10 gr.		
Brom. Camphor., ⅓ gr.		
Pv. Capsici, ½ gr.		

PILLS.	BOTTLE. 100	500
Antisplenetic, ...	60	2 75
Med. prop.—Anti-splenetic. Dose, 2 to 4. Pv. Aloes Soc., 1 gr. Pv. Ammoniaci, ½ gr. Pv. Myrrhæ, ½ gr. Ext. Bryony, 1 gr.		
Aperient	85	4 00
Med. prop.—Aperient, Tonic. Dose, 1 to 2. Ext. Nuc. Vom., ¼ gr. Ext. Hyoscyami, ½ gr. Ext. Coloc. Co., 2 grs.		
Aperient. (Dr. Fordyce Barker.)...	1 00	4 75
Med. prop.—Aperient. Ext. Coloc. Co., 1⅔ gr. Ext. Nuc. Vom., ½ gr. Ext. Hyoscyam., 1¼ gr. Pulv. Ipecac, 1-12 gr. Pulv. Aloes Soc't, 5-12 gr. Res. Podophylli., 1-12 gr.		
Aperient. (Drysdale.)	60	2 75
Med. prop.—Aperient. Dose, 1 to 2. Pv. Rhei, 1¼ gr. Pv. Ipecac, 5-12 gr. Pv. Aloes Soc., 1¼ gr. Pv. Nuc. Vom., ½ gr.		
Arthrosia. (See special page)	80	
Med. prop.—Antilithic, Tonic, Alterative. Acid Salicylic. Ext. Colchicum. Ext. Phytolacca. Res. Podoyhylli. Quinine. Pv. Capsicum.		
Asafœtida, U. S. P.	40	1 75
Med. prop.—Nerve Stimulant. Dose, 1 to 3.		
Asafœtida, 2 grs	40	1 75
Med. prop.—Nerve Stimulant. Dose, 2 to 4.		
Asafœtida Comp.	40	1 75
Med. prop.—Tonic and Nerve Stimulant. Dose, 2 to 3. Asafœtidæ, 2 grs. Ferri Sulph. Exsic., 1 gr.		

12

PILLS.	BOTTLE.	
	100	500
Asafœtida et Aloes................ Med. prop.–Purgative, Anti-spasmodic. Dose, 2 to 5.	40	1 75
Asafœtida et Rhei............... Med. prop.—Tonic, Laxative, Nerve Stimulant. Dose, 2 to 4. Asafœtidæ, 1 gr. Pulv. Rhei, . 1 gr. Ferri Redact., 1 gr.	75	3 50
Astringent......................... Med. prop.—Astringent. Dose, 1 to 2. Ext. Geranii, 2 grs. Pv. Opii, ¾ gr. Ol. Menth. Pip., 1-20 gtt. Ol. Res. Zingiber., 1-20 gtt.	60	2 75
Atropina. 1-60 and 1-100 gr........ Med. prop.—Anodyne.	75	3 50
Atropinæ Sulph. 1-60 gr......... Med. prop.—Anodyne.	75	3 50
Bismuth Subcarb. 3 grs......... Med. prop.—Sedative. Dose, 2 to 5.	75	3 50
Bismuth Subnit. 3 grs.......... Med. prop.—Sedative, Anti-periodic. Dose, 1 to 5.	75	3 50
Bismuth et Ext. Nuc. Vom..... Med. prop.—Sedative, Tonic. Dose, 1 to 2. Bismuth. Subcarb., 4 grs. Ext. Nuc. Vomicæ, ¼ gr.	1 50	7 25
Bismuth et Ignatia............. Med. prop. — Sedative, Anti-periodic, Tonic. Dose, 1 to 2. Bismuth. Subcarb., 4 grs. Ext. Ignatiæ Amara, ¼ gr.	1 50	7 25
Blennorrhagie. (W & Co.)........ Dose, 1 to 2. Terebinth Alb., 1½ grs. Ext. Humuli, ¾ gr. Camph. Monobrom. ¾ gr. Res. Podophyllin, ½ gr. The remedy *par excellence* for Chronic Blennorrhœa, uncomplicated with organic stricture, very frequently effecting a speedy cure in gleet of long standing. It is also almost equally serviceable as a remedy for cystorrhœa and inflammation of whatever kind effecting the urinary or sexual organs.	1 00	4 75

PILLS.	BOTTLE.	
	1000	500
Caffein Citras. 1 gr..............	2 75	3 50
Med. prop.—Nerve Stimulant. Dose, 1.		
Calcium Sulphide. 1-10 gr.......	50	2 25
Med. prop.—Useful in Cutaneous Diseases. Dose, 2 to 4.		

[EXTRACT FROM DR. HOWARD CANE'S ARTICLE IN THE LONDON LANCET.]

From the great frequency of occurrence of acne, and from its manifesting itself on the faces of individuals of both sexes, any therapeutic agent which promises success in this often intractable skin disease will be welcomed by most practitioners. I do not bring the sulphide of calcium forward as a new remedy in the treatment of this disease, for it was recommended some years ago by Dr. Sydney Ringer, but I wish to bring it more prominently into notice as a drug which will often prove of signal service in acne when other means have failed. The success which I attained in my first case which was of a most obstinate nature, led me to try it in others.

Calcium Sulphide. ¼ gr........	60	2 75
Med. prop.—Useful in Cutaneous Diseases. Dose, 2 to 3.		
Calcium Sulphide. ½ gr........	75	3 50
Med. prop.—Useful in Cutaneous Diseases. Dose, 2 to 3.		
Calcium Sulphide. 1 gr..........	1 00	4 75
Med. prop.—Useful in Cutaneous Diseases. Dose, 1 to 2.		
Calomel. ½ gr., 1, 2, and 3 grs......	40	1 75
Med. prop.—Alterative. Dose, 1 to 3.		
Calomel. 5 grs....................	50	2 25
Med. prop.—Alterative, Purgative. Dose, 1 to 3.		
Calomel et Opii.................	85	4 00
Med. prop.—Cathartic, Anodyne. Dose 1		

Calomel,   2 grs. }
Opium,   1 gr. }

Calomel et Rhei...............	75	3 50
Med. prop.—Mild Purgative. Dose, 1 to 3.		

Calomel,   ⅓ gr. }
Ext. Rhei,   ½ gr. }
Ext. Coloc. Comp.,   ½ gr. }
Ext. Hyoscyami,   ⅙ gr. }

14

PILLS.	BOTTLE.	
	100	500
Camphor. ¼ gr................ Med. prop.—Diaphoretic Carminative. Dose, 2 to 4.	40	1 75
Camphor. 1 gr................ Med. prop.—Diaphoretic, Carminative. Dose, 1 to 2.	50	2 25
Camphor et Ext. Hyoscyamus Med. prop.—Anodyne, Cerebral Stimulant. Dose, 1 to 2. Camphor, 1 gr. } Ext. Hyoscyami, Eng., 1 gr. }	50	2 25
Camphor Monobromated. 2 grs. Med. prop.—Anti-spasmodic. Dose, 1 to 2.	1 50	7 25
Cascara Comp................ Med. prop.—Laxative, Cathartic. Ext. Cascara Sagrad., 3 grs. } Res. Podophylli., ⅛ gr. }	75	3 50
Cathart. Comp., U. S. P........ Med. prop.—Cathartic. Dose, 2 to 4. These pills are made strictly in accordance with the formula as directed by the Pharmacopœia.	50	2 25
Cathart. Comp., Imprv'd...... Med. prop.—Cathartic. Dose, 2 to 4. Ext. Coloc. Comp. Ext. Jalap. Podophyllin, Leptandrin. Ext. Hyoscyami. Ext. Gentian. Ol. Menth. Pip.	50	2 25
Cathart. Comp., Vegetable.... Med. prop.—Cathartic. Dose, 2 to 3. Podophyllin, Scammony. Ext. Colocynth. Aloes, Soap, and Cardamom.	50	2 25
Cathart. Comp., Cholagogue.. Med. prop.—Cathartic. Dose, 2 to 4. Res. Podophylli, ½ gr. Pil. Hydrarg., ¼ gr. Ext. Hyoscyami, ⅛ gr. Ext. Nuc. Vom., 1-16 gr. Ol. Res. Capsici, ⅛ gtt.	60	2 75
Caulophyllin. 1-10 gr......... Med. prop.—Emmenagogue. Dose, 1 to 3.	40	1 75

15

PILLS.	BOTTLE.	
	100	500

Chalybeate. 3 grs. 60

Med. prop.—Antichlorotic.

   Ferri Sulph.,   1½ gr. }
   Potassa Carb.,   1½ gr. }

This combination which we have successfully and scientifically put in pill form produces when taken into the stomach, Carbonate of Protoxide of Iron, (Ferrous Carbonate) in a quickly assimilable condition.

This pill contributed to make the reputation of Niemeyer, and the following language, which speaks without comment, is taken from his TEXT BOOK ON THE PRACTICE OF MEDICINE.

PROF. NIEMEYER says: "For more than twenty years I have used these pills almost exclusively in Chlorosis, and have witnessed such brilliant results from them in a large number of cases that I have never needed any opportunity to experiment with other articles. At Madgeburg and Greifswald I often had to send my recipe for the pills to a great distance, my good fortune in the treatment of Chlorosis —to which, by-the-by, I owe the rapid growth of my practice—having given me great repute as the possessor of a sovereign remedy against that disease."

The dose of Pil. Chalybeate is from 1 to 4 at meal times and is recommended and successfully used in the treatment of Pulmonary Phthisis or Consumption, Anæmia and Chlorosis, Caries and Scrofulous Abscesses, Chronic Discharges, Dyspepsia, Loss of Appetite, etc.

The physician may see that he is obtaining exactly what he prescribes, by ordering in bottles containing 100 each.

Ceril Oxalas. 1 gr. .... 1 00 | 4 75

Med. prop.—Nerve Tonic. Dose, 1 to 3.

Chapman's Dinner Pills ...... 60 | 2 75

Med. prop.—Stimulating, Laxative. Dose, 1 to 3.

     Pulv. Aloes Soc.
     Pulv. Rhei Opt.
     Gum Mastich.

Chinoidin. 1 gr. .... 40 | 1 75

Med. prop.—Tonic, Anti-periodic. Dose, 2 to 4.

16

PILLS.	BOTTLE.	
	100	500
Chinoidin. 2 grs................	50	2 25
Med. prop.—Tonic, Anti-periodic.		
Dose, 2 to 4.		
Chinoidin Comp................	75	3 50
Med. prop.—Tonic, Anti-periodic.		
Dose, 1 to 2.		
Chinoidin, 2 grs. ⎫		
Ferri Sulph. Exsic., 1 gr. ⎬		
Piperin, ½ gr. ⎭		
Cholagogue. (Dr. Blackwood.)....	1 00	4 75
Med. prop.—"An admirable Cholago-		
gue." Dose, 1 to 2.		
Cinchonid. Sulph., ½ gr. ⎫		
Euonymin, ½ gr. ⎪		
Leptandrin, ½ gr. ⎪		
Iridin, ½ gr. ⎪		
Juglandin, ¼ gr. ⎬		
Podophyllin, ⅙ gr. ⎪		
Ext. Belladon., ⅙ gr. ⎪		
Ext. Nuc. Vom., ⅙ gr. ⎪		
Ext. Hyoscyam., ⅙ gr. ⎭		
Cinchofugin. 1-10 gr"..........	40	1 75
Med. prop.—Tonic, Nerve Stimulant.		
Dose, 1 to 4.		
Cinchoninæ Sulph. 1½ gr......	75	3 50
Med. prop.—Tonic, Anti-periodic.		
Dose, 1 to 3.		
Cinchoninæ Sulph. 2 grs.......	75	3 50
Med. prop.—Tonic, Anti-periodic.		
Dose, 1 to 3.		
Cinchonidin. Comp. (Warner &		
Co.).............................	1 50	7 25
Med. prop.—Tonic, Anti-periodic.		
Cinchonid. Sulph., 2 grs. ⎫		
Ac. Salicylic., 1 gr. ⎪		
Pv. Opii, ½ gr. ⎬		
Ol. Res. Capsici., ¼ gr. ⎭		
This pill is also termed Pil. Salicylic		
Acid Comp.		
Cinchonidinæ Salicylate. 2½	1 50	7 25
grs.............................		
Med. prop.—Anti-rheumatic. Dose, 1		
to 2.		
Cinchonidinæ Sulph. 1 gr......	45	2 00
Med. prop.—Anti-malarial, Anti-perio-		
dic. Dose, 1 to 3.		

PILLS.	BOTTLE.	
	100	500
Cinchonidinæ Sulph. 2 grs.... Med. prop.—Anti-malarial, Anti-perio- dic. Dose, 1 to 3.	65	3 00
Cinchonidinæ Sulph. 3 grs .... Med. prop.—Anti-malarial, Anti-perio- dic. Dose, 1 to 2.	90	4 25
Cinchonidinæ Sulph. 5 grs..... Med. prop.—Anti-periodic, Anti-mala- rial. Dose, 1 to 2.	1 50	7 25
Cincho-Quinine. 1 gr. .... Med. prop.—Tonic, Anti-periodic. Dose, 1 to 3.	1 00	4 75
Cincho-Quinine. 2 grs........... Med. prop.—Tonic, Anti-periodic. Dose, 1 to 2.	1 90	9 25
Coccia........................... Med. prop.—Hydragogue cathartic. Dose, 2 to 4. Pulv. Res. Scammon., 1 gr. Pulv. Soc. Aloes, 1¼ gr. Pulv. Colocynth., ½ gr. Potass. Sulph., ⅓ gr. Ol. Caryophyl., ⅛ gtt.	90	4 25
Codein. ¼ gr...................... Med. prop.—Anodyne, replacing mor- phine without the usual disagreeable after-effects produced by the latter. Dose, 1 to 2.	1 25	6 00
Colocynthidis Comp., U. S. P. 3 grs............................. Med. prop.—Purgative. Dose, 2 to 5.	80	3 75
Colocynth. et Hydrarg. et Ipe- **cac**............................... Med. prop.—Cholagogue, Cathartic. Dose, 1 to 3. Pulv. Ext. Coloc. Co., 2 grs. Pil. Hydrarg., 2 grs. Pulv. Ipecac, ⅛ gr.	75	3 50
Colocynth. et Hyoscyamus. ... Med. prop.—Gentle laxative. Dose, 1 to 2. Ext. Coloc. Comp., 2½ grs. Ext. Hyoscyami, 1½ gr.	75	3 50

PILLS.	BOTTLE.	
	100	500
Cook's 3 Grs.............................	50	2 25
Med. prop.—Purgative. Dose, 2 to 4.		
Pulv. Aloes Soc., 1 gr.		
Pulv. Rhei, 1 gr.		
Calomel, ⅓ gr.		
Sapon. Hispan., ½ gr.		
Copaibæ, U. S. P...................	50	2 25
Med. prop. — Alterative to Mucous		
Membrane. Dose, 2 to 6.		
Copaibæ et Ext. Cubebæ........	80	3 75
Med. prop.—Alterative to Mucous		
Membrane. Dose, 2 to 4.		
Pil. Copaibæ, 3 grs.		
Oleo-Resin Cubebæ, 1 gr.		
Copaibæ Comp....................	80	3 75
Med. prop — Alterative to Mucous		
Membrane, Tonic. Dose, 2 to 4.		
Pil. Copaib.		
Resin. Guaiac.		
Ferri Citras.		
Oleo-Resin. Cubebæ.		
Corrosive Sublimate. 1-12, 1-20,		
1-40 and 1-100 gr..................	40	1 75
Med. prop.—Mercurial, Alterative.		
Corrosive Sublimate has been adminis-		
tered with most gratifying results in		
certain forms of Chronic Dyspepsia.		
Ringer and other eminent therapeutists		
extol it very highly in 1-100 gr. doses in		
dysentery of children, regarding it as		
almost specific.		
Damianæ cum Phos. et Nuc.		
Vom................................	1 50	
Med. prop —Aphrodisiac. Dose, 1 to 2.		
Ext. Damianæ, 2 grs.		
Phosphori, 1-100 gr.		
Ext. Nuc. Vom., ½ gr.		
A valuable remedy indicated in sexual		
debility, over work of the brain, impo-		
tency, etc. It is also highly recommended		
as an uterine tonic. Also of value in		
Leucorrhœa, Amenorrhœa, Dysmenorr-		
hœa, etc.		
Diaphoretic........	75	3 50
Med. prop.—Diaphoretic. Dose, 1 to 2.		
Morphiæ Acetas., 1-25 gr.		
Pv. Ipecac, ¼ gr.		
Pv. Potass. Nitras., 1 gr.		
Pv. Camphoræ, ⅛ gr.		

19

PILLS.	BOTTLE.	
	100	500

Digestiva 75

Med. prop.—Useful in Indigestion.
Dose, 1 to 2.

Pepsin Concentrat.,	1 gr.
Pv. Nuc. Vom.,	¼ gr.
Gingerine,	1-½ gr.
Sulphur,	⅛ gr.

This combination is very useful in relieving various forms of Dyspepsia and Indigestion and will afford permanent benefit in cases of enfeebled digestion, where the gastric juices are not properly secreted.

As a corrective of nausea or lack of appetite in the morning, induced by over indulgence in food or stimulants during the night, these pills are unsurpassed; they should be taken in doses of two pills before retiring or in the morning at least one hour before eating; the first mentioned time is the most desirable as the effects are more decided, owing to the longer period for action and the natural rest is more fully experienced through their mild but effective influence.

As a dinner pill, Pil: Digestiva is unequalled and may be taken in doses of a single pill either before or after eating.

Digitalin. (Alkaloid.) 1-60 gr. ...... 75 | 3 50

Med. prop.—Arterial sedative. Dose, 1 to 2.

Digitalis Comp. .... 50 | 2 25

Med. prop.—Arterial sedative. Dose, 1 to 3.

Pv. Digitalis,	1 gr.
Pv. Scilla,	1 gr.
Potass. Nitras.,	2 grs.

Diuretic .... 50 | 2 25

Med. prop.—Diuretic, Antacid. Dose, 1 to 3.

Sapon. Hispan. Pv.,	2 grs.
Sodii Carb. Exsic.,	2 grs.
Ol. Baccæ Junip.,	1 gtt.

Dupuytren .... 50 | 2 25

Med. prop.—Specific Alterative. Dose, 1.

Pulv. Guaiac.,	3 grs.
Hydg. Chlor. Cor.,	1-10 gr.
Pulv. Opii,	⅛ gr.

PILLS.	BOTTLE.	
	100	500
Eccoprotic........................	60	2 75
Med. prop.—Mild cathartic. Dose, 2		
to 4.		
Ext. Aloes Soc., 2 grs.		
Ext. Nuc. Vomicæ, 1-5 gr.		
Res. Podophylli, 5-10 gr.		
Ol. Caryophyl., 1-10 gtt.		
Elaterium. (Clutterbuck's) 1-10 gr.	95	4 50
Med. prop.—Diuretic, Hydragogue		
Cathartic. Dose, 1 to 2.		
Emmenagogue	1 25	6 00
Med. prop.—Active Emmenagogue,		
Tonic. Dose, 1 to 3.		
Ergotine, 1 gr.		
Ext. Hellebor. Nig., 1 gr.		
Aloes, 1 gr.		
Ferri Sul. Exs., 1 gr.		
Ol. Sabinæ, ½ gr.		
Emmenagogue. (Matter)...........	40	1 75
Med. prop.—Emmenagogue. Dose, 1		
to 3.		
Ferri Sulph. Exs., 1½ gr.		
Aloes Pv., ½ gr.		
Terebinth. Alb., 1½ gr.		
Ergotin. 1 gr........................	1 00	4 75
Med. prop.—Parturient.		
Ergotin. 3 grs.......................	1 50	7 25
Med. prop.—Parturient.		
Dose, 1 to 2.		
Ergotin. Comp. (Dr. Reeves.)....	1 75	8 50
Med. prop.—Sedative, Parturient.		
Ergotin, 3 grs.		
Ext. Cannab. Ind., ¼ gr.		
Ext. Belladon., ¼ gr.		
Extract Belladonna. (Eng.) ¼ gr.	40	1 75
Med. prop.—Anodyne.		
Extract Cannabis Indica. ¼ gr.	60	2 75
Med. prop.—Anodyne.		
Ext. Guaranæ. 3 grs.............	2 00	9 75
Med. prop.—Nervine. Dose, 1 to 3.		
Extract Hyoscyamus. (Eng.)		
½ gr............................	40	1 75
Med. prop.—Nerve Stimulant.		
Ext. Coca. 3 grs..................	80	3 75
Med. prop.—A powerful Tonic and		
Sedative. Dose, 1 to 2.		

PILLS.	BOTTLE.	
	100	500
Extract Ignatia Amara. ¼ gr.	50	2 25
Med. prop.—Nerve Sedative. Dose, 1 to 2.		
Extract Nuc. Vom. ¼ and ½ gr..	40	1 75
Med. prop.—Nerve Stimulant. Dose, 1 to 3.		
Fel Bovinum...................	50	2 25
Med. prop.—Laxative. Dose, 1 to 3.		
Fel Bovis. Ins. 2 grs. }		
Pv. Zingiber Jam., 1 gr. }		
Ferri Iodid. 1 gr...........	80	
Med. prop.—Tonic, Alterative. Dose, 1 to 2.		

In cases where Iodide of Iron is prescribed, it is absolutely necessary, for the physician, who relies on the therapeutic action for beneficial results, that the compound should be perfectly protected, and so prepared as to remain inalterable and stable.

With this important fact in view, we have devoted special study to Iodide of Iron in pilular form, and are warranted in announcing that Warner & Co.'s Iodide of Iron Pills meet all the requirements, and are the most perfect preparation of the kind.

A salt is formed and so prepared as to guard against oxidation, and will remain unchanged for years. A coating of pure sugar renders them pleasant to administer, and further insures protection.

In proof of the above statement, a pill cut through presents all the characteristics of a perfect pill mass and the presence of Iodide Iron, without the free Iodine, forming a clear solution; and dissolving *readily* if thrown into a glass of water.

The dose of Iodide Iron Pills is from ONE to TWO at meal time and is recommended and successfully used in the treatment of Pulmonary Phthisis or Consumption, Anœmia and Chlorosis, Caries and Scrofulous Abscesses, Chronic Discharges, Dyspepsia, Loss of Appetite, etc.

Ferri Carb. (Vallett's) **U. S. P.**		
3 grs........................	40	1 75
Med. prop.—Tonic. Dose, 1 to 4.		

PILLS.	BOTTLE.	
	100	500
Ferri Citras, U. S. P. 2 grs......	50	2 25
Med. prop.—Tonic. Dose, 1 to 3.		
Ferri Comp., U. S. P............	40	1 75
Med. prop.—Tonic, Emmenagogue. Dose, 2 to 6.		
Ferri Lactas. 1 gr.............	50	2 25
Med. prop.—Tonic. Dose, 1 to 3.		
Ferri Pyrophos. 1 gr...........	40	1 75
Med. prop.—Tonic. Dose, 1 to 3.		
Ferri et Quas. et Nuc. Vom....	75	3 50
Med. prop.—Tonic, Nerve Stimulant. Dose. 1 to 2.		
Fer. per Hydrog., 1½ gr.		
Ext. Quassia, 1 gr.		
Ext. Nuc. Vom., ¼ gr.		
Pulv. Saponis, ½ gr.		
Ferri et Strychnin..............	75	3 50
Med. prop.—Tonic, Nerve stimulant. Dose, 1 to 2.		
Ferrum per Hydrog., 2 grs.		
Strychninæ, 1-60 gr.		
Ferri et Strychninæ Cit........	75	3 50
Med. prop.—Tonic, Nerve stimulant. Dose, 1 to 2.		
Strych. Citras., 1-50 gr.		
Ferri Citras., 1 gr.		
Ferri Sulph. Exs. 2 grs.........	40	1 75
Med. prop.—Tonic. Dose, 2 to 4.		
Ferri Valer. 1 gr................	1 00	4 75
Med. prop.—Tonic, Anti-spasmodic. Dose, 1 to 2.		
Ferrum. (Quevenne's.) 1 gr......	50	2 25
Med. prop.—Tonic. Dose, 1 to 3.		
Ferrum. (Quevenne's.) 2 grs......	75	3 50
Med. prop.—Tonic. Dose, 1 to 2.		
Galbani Comp.........	50	2 25
Med. prop.—Anti-spasmodic. Dose, 2 to 4.		
Galbani, 1½ gr.		
Pv. Myrrh., ½ gr.		
Asafœt, ½ gr.		
Gambogiæ Comp................	40	1 75
Med. prop.—Active purgative. Dose, 2 to 5.		
Pv. Gambogia.		
Pv. Aloes Socot.		
Pv. Zingib. Jam.		
Pv. Saponis. [23]		

PILLS.	BOTTLE.	
	100	500
Gelsemin. 1-16 gr....................	40	1 75
Med. prop.—Arterial sedative. Dose, 1 to 4.		
Gelsemin. ⅛ gr....................	50	2 25
Med. prop.—Arterial sedative. Dose, 1 to 2.		
Gelsemin. ¼ gr....................	75	3 50
Med. prop.—Arterial Sedative. Dose, 1 to 2.		
Gentian. Comp. (Aloe Comp.)....	40	1 75
Med. prop.—Tonic, Purgative. Dose, 2 to 4.		
Ext. Gentian, ⅖ gr. ⎫		
Pv. Aloes Soc., 2 grs. ⎬		
Ol. Carui, 1-5 gr. ⎭		
Gonorrhœa......................	60	2 75
Med. prop.—Tonic, Alterative to Mucous Membrane. Dose, 1 to 3.		
Pulv. Cubeb., 2 grs. ⎫		
Bals. Copaib. Solid., 1 gr. ⎪		
Ferri Sulph., ¼ gr. ⎬		
Terebinth. Venet., 1½ gr. ⎭		
Heim's (Niemeyer.)...............	1 25	6 00
Med. prop.—Anti-periodic, Tonic. Dose, 1.		
Quinine Sulph., 1 gr. ⎫		
Pulv. Digital. Fol., ½ gr. ⎪		
Pulv. Ipecac, ¼ gr. ⎬		
Pulv. Opii, ¼ gr. ⎭		
Helonin. 1-10 gr....................	50	2 25
Med. prop.—Cathartic. Dose, 1 to 4.		
Hepatica......................	80	3 75
Med. prop.—Cholagogue, Cathartic. Dose, 1 to 2.		
Pil. Hydrarg., 3 grs. ⎫		
Ext. Coloc. Comp., 1 gr. ⎬		
Ext. Hyoscyami, 1 gr. ⎭		
Hooper. (Female Pills.) 2¼ grs....	40	1 75
Med. prop.–Emmenagogue. Dose, 1 to 3		
Hydrarg. 5 grs....................	50	2 25
Med. prop.—Mercurial alterative. Dose, 1 to 2.		
Hydrargyri. U. S. P. 3 grs......	40	1 75
Med. prop.—Mercurial alterative. Dose, 2 to 3.		
Hydrarg. Bin Iodide. 1-16 gr....	40	1 75
Med. prop.—Alterative. Dose, 1 to 3.		

PILLS.	BOTTLE.	
	100	500
Hydrargyri Comp............	75	3 50
Med. prop.—Mercurial alterative.		
Dose, 1 to 2.		
Mass. Hydrarg., 1 gr. ⎫		
Pulv. Opii, ½ gr. ⎬		
Pulv. Ipecac, ¼ gr. ⎭		
Hydrargyri Iod. et Opii.		
(Ricords.)....................	75	3 50
Med. prop.—Mercurial alterative.		
Dose, 1 to 2.		
Hydrarg. Iodid., 1 gr. ⎫		
Pulv. Opii, ⅓ gr. ⎬		
Hydrarg. Prot Iodide. 1-5 gr..	40	1 75
Med. prop.—Alterative. Dose, 1 to 4.		
Our preparation of Prot Iodid. Mercury is made by precipitation and is entirely free from traces of the Bin-Iodid.		
Hydrarg. Prot Iodide. ⅛ gr...	40	1 75
Med. prop.—Alterative. Dose, 1 to 4.		
Hydrarg. Prot Iodide. ¼ gr...	40	1 75
Med. prop.—Alterative. Dose, 1 to 2.		
Hydrarg. Prot Iodide. ½ gr...	50	2 25
Med. prop.—Alterative. Dose, 1 to 2.		
Hydrastin. ⅛ gr................	95	4 50
Med. prop.—Cathartic. Dose, 1 to 2.		
Hyoscyamiæ. 1-100 gr...........	3 00	14 75
(Crystals, Pure Alkaloid.)		
Med. prop.—Anodyne, Soporific.		
Dose, 1.		
Iodoform. 1 gr.................	1 00	4 75
Med. prop.—Tonic, Alterative. Dose, 1 to 2.		
Iodoform et Ferri.............	1 50	
Med. prop.—Tonic, Alterative. Dose, 1 to 2.		
Iodoform, 1 gr. ⎫		
Ferri Redact., 1¼ gr. ⎬		
Iodoform et Ferri et Nuc. Vom	1 50	
Med. prop.—Tonic, Alterative. Dose, 1 to 2.		
Iodoform, 1 gr. ⎫		
Ferri Redact., 1 gr. ⎬		
Ext. Nuc. Vom., ¼ gr. ⎭		

25

PILLS.	BOTTLE.	
	100	500

Iodoform et Hydrarg 1 50
Med. prop.—Alterative, Dose, 1 to 3.
  Iodoform,   ½ gr. }
  Hydrarg. Prot Iodid.,   ¼ gr. }

Iodoform et Nuc. Vom. Comp. 1 50
Med. prop.—Alterative, Tonic, Laxative, Repellant. Dose, 1 to 3.
  Iodoform   ½ gr.]
  Ext. Nuc. Vom.,   ⅓ gr.]
  Podophyllin,   1-16 gr.]
  Ext. Belladon.,   ⅛ gr.]

Iodoform et Quinine 1 25
Med. prop.—Alterative, Tonic. Dose, 1 to 3.
  Iodoform,   ½ gr. }
  Quininæ Bisulph.,   ½ gr. }

Iodoform et Quinina et Ferri 1 75   8 50
Med. prop.—Tonic, Alterative. Dose, 1 to 2.
  Iodoform,   1 gr. }
  Ferri Carb., (Vallet's)   2 grs. }
  Quininæ Sul.,   ½ gr. }

Iodoform therapeutically is alterative, nervine, sorbefacient, anti-periodic, and anæsthetic. As an alterative it acts with more rapidity than other medicines of that class, in doses of one, two, or three grains, repeated thrice daily. As a nervine it is prompt and efficient; while it gives nervous strength, it calms speedily the most severe pains.

It is rapidly absorbed into the blood.

Accumulative effects have not been observed.

Iodoform is destitute of any local irritant action, and has that advantage over all other iodic remedies.

It may be administered, with reasonable expectation of success, in the following diseases:

Neuralgia of every description, chronic rheumatism, consumption, scrofula, ophthalmia, chronic ulcerations, and skin diseases, syphilis, and certain affections of the neck of the bladder and prostrate gland, and whenever a powerful alterative agent is needed. This quality of Iodoform is greatly enchanced, in the majority of cases, by the addition of pure iron, Fer. per hydrog.

PILLS.	BOTTLE. 100	500
Ipecac. et Opii. 3⅓ grs. (Pulv. Doveri, U. S. P.)........	50	2 25
Med. prop.—Anodyne, Soporific. Dose, 1 to 3.		
Ipecac. et Opii. 5 grs........	65	3 00
Med. prop.—Anodyne, Soporific. Dose 1.		
Irisin Comp........	50	2 25
Med. prop.—Cathartic, Nerve stimulant. Dose, 1 to 2.		
Irisin, ¼ gr. / Podophyllin, 1-10 gr. / Strychnine, 1-40 gr.		
Laxative........	60	2 75
Med. prop.—Gentle purgative. Dose, 1 to 2.		
Pulv. Aloes Soc., 1 gr. / Sulphur, 1-5 gr. / Res. Podophylli, 1-5 gr. / Res. Guaiaci, ½ gr. / Syr. Rhamni, q. s.		
Leptandrin. ¼ gr........	40	1 75
Med. prop. Cathartic. Dose, 1 to 4.		
Leptandrin. ½ gr........	50	2 25
Med. prop.—Cathartic. Dose, 1 to 2.		
Leptandrin. 1 gr........	75	3 50
Med. prop.—Cathartic. Dose, 1.		
Leptandrin Comp........	1 00	4 75
Med. prop.—Laxative, Diuretic. Dose, 1 to 2.		
Leptandrin, 1 gr. / Irisin ¼ gr. / Podophyllin, ⅛ gr.		
Lupulin. 3 grs........	40	1 75
Med. prop.—Anodyne. Dose, 2 to 4.		
Morphinæ Acetas. ⅛ gr........	70	3 25
Med. prop.—Anodyne. Dose, 1 to 2.		
Morphinæ Comp........	1 25	6 00
Med. prop.—Anodyne, Febrifuge. Dose, 1.		
Morph. Sulph., ¼ gr. / Ant. et Pot. Tart., ¼ gr. / Hydrarg. Chlor. Mit., ¼ gr.		
Morphinæ Sulph. 1-20 gr........	40	1 75
Med. prop.—Anodyne. Dose, 1 to 2.		
Morphinæ Sulph. 1-10 gr........	50	2 25
Med. prop.—Anodyne. Dose, 1 to 2.		

PILLS.	BOTTLE.	
	100	500
Morphinæ Sulph. ⅛ gr...........	60	2 75
Med. prop.—Anodyne. Dose, 1 to 2.		
Morphinæ Sulph. ⅙ gr.........	70	3 25
Med. prop.—Anodyne. Dose, 1 to 2.		
Morphinæ Sulph. ¼ gr.........	90	4 25
Med. prop.—Anodyne. Dose, 1 to 2.		
Morphinæ Sulph. ½ gr.........	1 30	7 25
Med. prop.—Anodyne. Dose, 1.		
Morphinæ Valerianas. ⅛ gr...	90	4 25
Med. prop.—Anodyne. Dose, 1 to 2.		
Neuralgic.............................	2 50	12 25
Med. prop.—Tonic, Alterative, Anodyne. Dose, 1 to 3.		
Quininæ Sulph., 2 grs.		
Morphinæ Sulph., 1-20 gr.		
Strychnine, 1-30 gr.		
Acid Arsenious, 1-20 gr.		
Ext. Aconiti, ½ gr.		
Neuralgic. (One-half size.).........	1 50	7 25
Med. prop.—As above. Dose, 1 to 3.		
Neuralgic. (Brown Sequard.)........	2 00	9 75
Med. prop.—Anodyne. Dose, 1.		
Ext. Hyoscyami, ⅔ gr.		
Ext. Conii, ⅔ gr.		
Ext. Ignat. Amar., ½ gr.		
Ext. Opii, ½ gr.		
Ext. Aconiti, ⅓ gr.		
Ext. Cannab. Ind., ¼ gr.		
Ext. Stramon., 1-5 gr.		
Ext. Belladon., ⅙ gr.		
Neuralgic. (Sine Morphine.)........	2 50	12 25
Med. prop.—Tonic, Alterative. Dose, 1 to 3.		
Opii. ½ gr............................	40	1 75
Med. prop.—Anodyne. Dose, 1 to 2.		
Opii. U. S. P. 1 gr.................	50	2 25
Med. prop.—Anodyne. Dose, 1.		
Opii et Camphor....................	60	2 75
Med. prop.—Anodyne, Nerve sedative. Dose, 1.		
Pulv. Opii, 1 gr.		
Camphoræ, 2 grs.		

PILLS.	BOTTLE.	
	100	500

Opii et Camphor et Tannin ... 60 | 2 25
Med. prop.—Anodyne, Astringent.
Dose, 1 to 3.
Pulv. Opii, ¼ gr. ⎫
Camphoræ, 1 gr. ⎬
Acid Tannic, 2 grs. ⎭

Opii et Plumbi Acetas .... 50 | 2 25
Med. prop.—Anodyne, Sedative. Dose,
1 to 2.
Pulv. Opii, ½ gr. ⎫
Plumbi Acet., 1½ gr. ⎭

Opium. Purified. ½ gr .... 50 | 2 25
Med. prop.—Anodyne, Soporific. Dose,
1 to 2.

Phosphori. 1-100 gr., 1-50 gr., 1-25
gr., in each...................... 1 00
Med. prop.—Nerve stimulant. Dose, 1.

The method of preparing Phosphorus
in pilular form has been *discovered and
brought to perfection by us*, without the
necessity of combining it with resin, which
forms an insoluble compound. The element is in a perfect state of subdivision
and incorporated with the excipient while
in solution. The non-porous coating of
sugar protects it thoroughly from oxidation, so that the pill is not impaired by
age. It is the most pleasant and acceptable form for the administration of Phosphorus.

Phosphori Comp. 1 25
Med. prop.—Nerve tonic. Dose, 1.
Phosphori, 1-100 gr. ⎫
Ext. Nuc. Vom., ¼ gr. ⎭

**Phosphori cum Aloe et Nuc.
Vomica**...................... 1 50
Med. prop.—Useful in the atonic form
of Dyspepsia and Neurosis of the Stomach.
Dose, 1.
Phosphori, 1-50 gr. ⎫
Ext. Aloe Aq., ½ gr. ⎬
Ext. Nuc. Vom., ¾ gr. ⎭

Phosphori cum Belladonna. .. 1 50
Med. prop.—Useful in Anæmic Condi-
tions and Neuralgia. Dose, 1 to 2.
Phosphori, 1-100 gr. ⎫
Ext. Belladonna, ⅛ gr. ⎭

PILLS.	BOTTLE.	
	100	500

Phosphori cum Cannab. Ind. | 1 | 75 |

Med. prop.—Narcotic, Aphrodisiac.
Dose, 1 to 2.

Phosphori, 1-50 gr. }
Ext. Cannab. Ind., ¼ gr. }

Phosphori cum Ferro Comp. | 1 | 50 |

Med. prop.—Nutritive, Tonic and Stimulant to the Nervous system. Dose, 1.

Phosphori, 1-50 gr. }
Strychnine, 1-60 gr. }
Ferri Redact., 1½ gr. }

PHOSPHORUS has recently been prescribed with great advantage in cases of extreme debility and mental depression, from prolonged anxiety or excessive excitement; also, in nervous prostration from overwork, especially brain-work. It is recommended in cases which are attended with great prostration of the vital powers; in exhausting diseases, such as Cholera, Diphtheria, and the latter stages of Typhus and other Fevers, etc. In Epilepsy, Epileptiform-Vertigo, Melancholia, Softening and some other diseases of the Brain, it has been given with marked benefit; also in Neuralgia, Tuberculosis, and Scrofula, in chronic and inveterate diseases of the skin, Leprosy, Lupus, and Psoriasis. Dr. Burgess recommends it in Pruritus Pudendi and other forms of Pruritus.

PHOSPHORUS, STRYCHNINE, AND IRON, combined in the proportions above indicated, is a safe and valuable remedy. As a nutritive tonic and stimulant to the nervous system, especially the spinal cord, it is admirably adapted for the treatment of a large number of nervous disorders dependent on defective nutrition and debility. It increases appetite and promotes digestion. It may be safely given in all those cases in which hypophosphites are employed. It is strongly recommended in *Consumption, Neuralgia, Atonic Dyspepsia, Lowness of Spirit, in General Debility*, and in that general condition of depression and loss of power popularly known as *below par*, and in *breakdown* from overwork and mental fatigue.

PILLS.	BOTTLE.	
	100	500
Phosphori cum Digital. Co ...	1 50	
Med. prop.—Valuable as a Heart tonic.		
Dose, 1.		
Phosphori, 1-50 gr. ⎫		
Pv. Digitalis, 1 gr. ⎬		
Ext. Hyoscy., 1 gr. ⎭		
Phosphori cum Digitale et Ferro	1 50	
Med. prop.—Valuable as a Heart tonic.		
Dose, 1.		
Phosphori, 1-50 gr. ⎫		
Pv. Digitalis, 1 gr. ⎬		
Ferri Redact., 1 gr. ⎭		
Phosphori cum Ext. Aconiti ..	1 50	
Med. prop.—Useful in the Treatment		
of Phthisis with Pyrexia. Dose, 1.		
Phosphori, 1-50 gr. ⎫		
Ext. Aconiti, 1-16 gr. ⎭		
Phosphori cum Ferro	1 25	
Med. prop.—A Powerful Nervine tonic		
and Blood restorer. Dose, 1 to 2.		
Phosphori, 1-50 gr. ⎫		
Ferri Redact., 1 gr. ⎭		
Phosphori cum Cantharide Co	1 50	
Med. prop.—Stimulating emmenagogue		
and Diuretic. Dose, 1 to 2.		
Phosphori, 1-50 gr. ⎫		
Pv. Nuc. Vom., 1 gr. ⎬		
Sol. Cantharidis Con., 1 m. ⎭		
Phosphori cum Ferro et Nuc. Vom	1 25	
Med. prop.—Nerve stimulant, Tonic.		
Dose, 1 to 2.		
Phosphori, 1-100 gr. ⎫		
Ferri Carb., 1 gr. ⎬		
Ext. Nuc. Vom., ¼ gr. ⎭		
Phosphori cum Ferro et Quinine	1 60	
Med. prop.—Nerve tonic. Dose, 1 to 2		
Phosphori, 1-100 gr. ⎫		
Ferri Carb., 1 gr. ⎬		
Quinina Sul., 1 gr. ⎭		
Phosphori cum Ferro et Quinine et Nuc. Vom	1 60	
Med. prop.—Nerve tonic. Dose, 1 to 2		
Phosphori, 1-100 gr. ⎫		
Ferri Carb., 1 gr. ⎬		
Quinina Sul., 1 gr. ⎬		
Ext. Nuc. Vom., ¼ gr. ⎭		

PILLS.	BOTTLE.	
	100	500

Phosphori cum Ferro et Strychnina................ 1 50
Med. prop.—Nerve tonic and Stimulant.
Dose, 1 to 2.
Phosphori, 1-100 gr.
Ferri Carb., 1 gr.
Strychnin, 1-60 gr.

Phosphori cum Morphina et Zinco Valer............. 2 00
Med. prop.—Nerve tonic and Sedative.
Dose, 1.
Phosphori, 1-50 gr.
Morphinæ Sul., 1-12 gr.
Zinci Valer, 1 gr.

Phosphori cum Nuc. Vomica.. 1 25
Med. prop.—Nerve tonic and Stimulant.
Dose, 1 to 2.
Phosphori, 1-50 gr.
Ext. Nuc., Vom., ¾ gr.

Phosphori cum Opio et Digital........................ 1 50
Med. prop.—Useful in Arresting Abnormal calorification. Dose, 1 to 2.
Phosphori, 1-50 gr.
Pv. Digitalis, ½ gr.
Pv. Ipecac., ¾ gr.
Pv. Opii, ¾ gr.

Phosphori cum Quinina....... 1 80
Med. prop.—Nerve tonic. Dose, 1 to 2
Phosphori, 1-50 gr.
Quininæ Sul., 1 gr.

Phosphori cum Quininæ Co.. 1 35
Med. prop.—Nerve tonic. Dose, 1.
Phosphori, 1-50 gr.
Ferri Redact, 1 gr.
Quininæ Sul., ½ gr.
Strychnin, 1-60 gr.

Phosphori cum Quinina et Ferro et Strychnina...... 1 60
Med. prop.—Powerful nerve stimulant.
Dose, 1.
Phosphori 1-100 gr.
Quininæ Sul., 1 gr.
Ferri Redact, 1 gr.
Strychnin, 1-60 gr.

PILLS.	BOTTLE.	
	100	500

Phosphori cum Quinina et Digitale Co. 1 35
Med. prop.—Valuable as a Sedative and Diuretic. Dose, 1 to 2.
Phosphori, 1-50 gr.
Quininæ Sul., ½ gr.
Pv. Digitalis, ½ gr.
Pv. Opii, ¼ gr.
Pv. Ipecac., ¼ gr.

Phosphori cum Quinina et Nuc Vom 1 60
Med. prop.—Nerve tonic. Dose, 1 to 2
Phosphori, 1-50 gr.
Quininæ Sul., 1 gr.
Ext. Nuc. Vom., ¼ gr.

Phosphori cum Strychnina ... 1 25
Med. prop.—Nerve tonic and Stimulant. Dose, 1.
Phosphori, 1-50 gr.
Strychnin, 1-60 gr.

Phosphori cum Zinco Co. 1 50
Med. prop.—Useful in Uterine disturbances, Leucorrhœa and Hysteria. Dose, 1 to 2.
Phosphori, 1-50 gr.
Zinci Sul., 1 gr.
Lupulin, 1 gr.

Phosphori et Damiana cum Nuc. Vom 1 50
Med. prop.—Aphrodisiac. Dose, 1 to 2.
Ext. Damiana, 2 grs.
Phosphori, 1-100 gr.
Ext. Nuc. Vom., ⅛ gr.

Podophyllin. 1-10 gr. .... 40 | 1 75
Med. prop.—Cathartic. Dose, 1 to 4.

Podophyllin. ¼ gr. .... 40 | 1 75
Med. prop.—Cathartic. Dose, 1 to 4.

Podophyllin. ½ gr. .... 50 | 2 25
Med. prop.—Cathartic. Dose, 1 to 2.

Podophyllin. 1 gr. .... 75 | 3 50
Med. prop.—Cathartic. Dose, 1.

33

PILLS.	BOTTLE. 100	500
Podophylli. (Dr. E. R. Squibb.)... Dose, 1 to 2. Res. Podophylli, ¼ gr.; Pv. Capsici, ½ gr.; Ext. Belladon., ⅛ gr.; Pv. Sacch. Lact., 1 gr.; Acacia and Glycerin., aa q. s. The composition of this pill is the same as Dr. Squibb's recipe, and for administration is preferable, being just as soluble and more elegant in appearance. Practical test for Solubility:—Suspend 3 of these pills in water and they will dissolve, coating included, as soon as the plain pills ready prepared. This is accomplished through our method of manipulation and coating, and physicians should not regard the prejudice against sugar-coated pills as applying to Wm. R. Warner & Co.'s manufacture.	75	3 50
Podophyllin et Bellad........ Med. prop.—Mild stimulating laxative. Dose, 1 to 3. Podophyllin, ¼ gr.; Ext. Bellad., ⅛ gr.; Ol. Res. Capsici, ¼ gr.; Saccharum Lact., 1 gr.	75	3 50
Podophyllin Comp............ Med. prop.—Cathartic and Tonic. Dose, 1 to 2. Podophyllin, ½ gr.; Ext. Hyoscyami, ⅛ gr.; Ext. Nuc. Vomicæ, 1-16 gr.	75	3 50
Podophyllin Comp. (Eclectic.).. Med. prop.—Purgative. Dose, 2 to 4. Podophyllin, ⅛ gr.; Leptandrin, 1-16 gr.; Juglandin, 1-16 gr.; Macrotin, 1-32 gr.; Ol. Res. Capsici, q. s.	75	3 50
Podophyl. et Hydrarg........ Med. prop.—Laxative. Dose, 2 to 4. Podophyllin, ¼ gr.; Pil. Hydrarg., 2 grs.	50	2 25
Podophyllin et Hyoscyamus. Med. prop.—Gentle cathartic. Dose, 1 to 2. Podophyllin, ½ gr.; Ext. Hyoscyami, ½ gr.	60	2 75

PILLS.	BOTTLE.	
	100	500
Podophyllotoxin. ⅛ gr..........	50	2 25
Med. prop.—Cathartic, without the nausea induced by Podophyllin. Dose, 1 to 2.		
Podophyllotoxin. ¼ gr..........	75	3 50
Med. prop.—Cathartic, without the nausea induced by Podophyllin. Dose, 1 to 2.		
Post-Partum. (Dr. Fordyce Barker.) Dose, 1.	1 00	4 75
Ext. Coloc. Comp., 1½ gr. Hydrarg. Chlor. Mit., 1½ gr. Ext. Hyoscyami, ⅓ gr. Ext. Nuc. Vom., ⅙ gr. Pulv. Aloes, ⅙ gr. Pulv. Ipecac,. ⅙ gr.		
Potass. Bromid. 1 gr....	75	3 50
Med. prop.—Nerve sedative. Dose, 2 to 5.		
Potass. Bromid. 5 grs...........	1 25	6 00
Med. prop.—Nerve sedative. Dose, 1 to 2.		
Potass. Iodid. (Merck's) 2 grs....	85	4 00
Med. prop.—Alterative. Dose, 1 to 3.		
Potass. Permanganas. ⅛ gr...	50	2 25
Med. prop.—DR. ROBERTS BARTHOLOW, Professor of Materia Medica and Therapeutics in the Jefferson Medical College of Philadelphia, says ("Permanganate of Potassium, its Action and Uses"):—		
"One of the most important therapeutical applications of permanganate of potassium, a recent discovery, is in the treatment of amenorrhœa. We owe this valuable improvement, as indeed many others, to Drs. Ringer and Murrell. They have shown that this remedy is remarkably certain when applied in suitable cases. Given in doses of two to five grains three times a day, for several days preceding the menstrual molimen, this *agent is quite sure to start the flow*. Dose, 2 to 5 grs.		
Potass. Permanganas. 1 gr....	75	3 50
Med. prop.—As above. Dose, 1 to 4.		
Potass. Permanganas. 2 grs....	1 00	4 75
Med. prop.—As above. Dose, 1 to 2.		

PILLS.	BOTTLE.	
	100	500
Prandil................................... Med. prop.—Stimulating purgative. Dose, 1 to 2. Ext. Aloe Aq., 1 gr. ⎱ Ext. Gentian, 2 grs. ⎰ Ext. Anthemid., 1 gr. Pv. Capsici, ¼ gr.	75	3 50
Quininæ Bi-Sulph. ½ gr......... Med. prop.—Tonic, Anti-periodic. Dose, 1 to 4.	45	2 00
Quininæ Bi-Sulph. 1 gr.......... Med. prop.—Tonic, Anti-periodic. Dose, 1 to 3.	60	2 75
Quininæ Bi-Sulph. 2 grs........ Med. prop.—Tonic, Anti-periodic. Dose, 1 to 3.	00	4 75
Quininæ Bi-Sulph. 3 grs........ Med. prop.—Tonic, Anti-periodic. Dose, 1 to 2.	1 45	7 00
Quininæ Bi-Sulph. 5 grs........ Med. prop.—Tonic, Anti-periodic. Dose, 1 to 2.	2 35	11 50
Quininæ Comp.................... Med. prop.—Tonic, Anti-periodic. Dose, 1 to 2. Quininæ Sulph., 1 gr. ⎱ Fer. Carb. (Vallett's), 2 grs. ⎰ Acid Arsenious, 1-60 gr.	1 00	4 75
Quininæ cum Capsicum........ Med. prop.—Anti-periodic, Stimulant. Dose, 1 to 3. Quininæ Sulph., 1 gr. ⎱ Capsicum, ¼ gr. ⎰	1 00	4 75
Quininæ et Ext. Bellad........ Med. prop.—Nerve tonic, Anti-periodic. Dose, 1 to 2. Quininæ Sulph., 1 gr. ⎱ Ext. Belladon., ¼ gr. ⎰	1 00	4 75
Quininæ et Ferri................ Med. prop.—Tonic, Anti-periodic. Dose, 1 to 2. Quininæ Sulph., 1 gr. ⎱ Ferrum per Hydrog., 1 gr. ⎰	1 00	4 75
Quininæ et Ferri Carb........ Med. prop.—Tonic, Anti-periodic. Dose, 1 to 2. Quininæ Sulph., 1 gr. ⎱ Fer. Carb. (Vallett's), 2 grs. ⎰	1 00	4 75

PILLS.	BOTTLE.	
	100	500
Quininæ et Ferri Cit. 1 gr....	55	2 50
Med. prop.—Tonic, Anti-periodic. Dose, 1 to 2.		
Quininæ et Ferri Cit. 2 grs....	90	4 25
Med. prop.—Tonic, Anti-periodic. Dose, 1 to 2.		
Quininæ et Fer. et Strych-nin	1 00	4 75
Med. prop.—Tonic, Anti-periodic. Dose, 1 to 2. Quininæ Sulph., 1 gr. Fer. Carb. (Vallett's), 2 grs. Strych. Sulph., 1-60 gr.		
Quininæ et Fer. et Strych. Phos	1 25	6 00
Med. prop.—Tonic, Anti-periodic. Dose, 1 to 2. Quininæ Phos., 1 gr. Ferri Phos., 1 gr. Strychninæ Phos., 1-60 gr.		
Quininæ et Ferri Valer. 2 gr..	2 00	9 75
Med. prop.—Tonic, Nerve sedative. Dose, 1 to 2.		
Quininæ et Hydrarg	1 25	6 00
Med. prop.—Tonic, Anti-periodic. Dose, 1 to 2. Quininæ Sulph., 1 gr. Mass. Hydrarg., 2 grs. Oleo-Res. Piper. Nig., ¼ gr.		
Quininæ et Iodoform	1 50	
Med. prop.—Tonic, Alterative. Dose, 1 to 3. Iodoform, ½ gr. Quininæ Bi-Sulph., ½ gr.		
Quininæ Iodoform et Fer	1 75	8 50
Med. prop.—Tonic, Alterative. Dose, 1 to 2. Iodoform, 1 gr. Fer. Carb. (Vallett's), 2 grs. Quininæ Sulph., ½ gr.		
Quininæ et Strychnin	1 00	4 75
Med. prop.—Tonic, Nerve stimulant. Dose, 1 to 2. Quininæ Sulph., 1 gr. Strychninæ, 1-60 gr.		

PILLS.	BOTTLE.	
	100	500
Quininæ et Strychniæ Comp...	1 25	6 00
Med. prop.—Tonic, Alterative. Dose, 1.		
Quininæ Sulph., 1 gr.		
Ferri per Hydrog., 1½ gr.		
Strychnine, 1-20 gr.		
Acid Arsenicus, 1-20 gr.		
Quininæ Sulph. ½ gr............	45	2 00
Med. prop.—Tonic, Anti-periodic.		
Dose, 1 to 4.		
Our Quinine Pills are manufactured from Powers & Weightman's Quinine, and other brands having an established reputation. An examination by a competent Chemist is made to verify our tests. Each Pill contained in packages to which our label is attached, is warranted to have the full complement of pure material as expressed thereon.		
Quininæ Sulph. 1 gr............	60	2 75
Med. prop.—Tonic, Anti-periodic.		
Dose, 1 to 3.		
Quininæ Sulph. 2 grs............	1 00	4 75
Med. prop.—Tonic, Anti-periodic.		
Dose, 1 to 3.		
Quininæ Sulph. 3 grs............	1 45	7 00
Med. prop.—Tonic, Anti-periodic.		
Dose, 1 to 2.		
Quininæ Sulph. 5 grs............	2 35	11 50
Med. prop.—Tonic, Anti-periodic.		
Dose, 1 to 2.		
Quininæ Valerianas. ½ gr.....	1 45	7 00
Med. prop.—Tonic, Nervine Dose, 1 to 2.		
Quinidinæ Sulph. 1 gr..........	1 15	5 50
Med. prop.—Anti-periodic. Dose, 1 to 3		
Quinidinæ Sulph. 2 grs........	2 15	10 50
Med. prop.—Anti-periodic. Dose, 1 to 3		
Quinidinæ Sulph. 3 grs........	3 25	16 00
Med. prop.—Anti-periodic. Dose, 1 to 2		
Rhei Comp., U. S. P............	75	3 50
Med. prop.—Purgative. Dose, 2 to 4.		
Pulv. Rhei, 2 grs.		
Pur. Aloes, 1½ gr.		
Myrrh., 1 gr.		
Ol. Menth. Pip., 1-10 gr.		

PILLS.	BOTTLE.	
	100	500

Rhei et Hydrarg..............
Med. prop.—Cholagogue cathartic.
  Dose, 2 to 5.
  Pulv. Rhei.
  Mass. Hydrarg.
  Sodii Carb. Exsic.
	80	3 75

Rhei, U. S. P.................
Med. prop.—Gentle laxative. Dose, 1
  to 5.
  Pulv. Rhei,   3 grs. }
  Pulv. Saponis,   1 gr. }
	75	3 50

Rheumatic.....................
Med. prop.—Anti-rheumatic, Purgative.
  Dose, 1 to 3.
  Ext. Coloc. Comp.,   1½ gr. }
  Ext. Colchici Acet.,   1 gr. }
  Ext. Hyoscyami,   ⅓ gr. }
  Hydrarg. Chlor. Mit., ⅔ gr. }
	90	4 25

Salicylic Acid. 2½ grs............ Med. prop.—Anti-rheumatic. Dose, 1 to 2.	75	3 50
Salicylic Acid. 5 grs............. Med. prop.—Anti-rheumatic. Dose, 1 to 2.	1 30	6 25
Santonin. 1 gr.................... Med. prop.—Anthelmintic. Dose, 1 to 3.	1 00	4 75

Scillæ Comp., U. S. P..........
Med. prop.—Expectorant, Diuretic.
  Dose, 1 to 3.
  Pulv. Scillæ,   ½ gr. }
  Pulv. Zingiber. Jam.,   1 gr. }
  Gum Ammoniac,   1 gr. }
  Pulv. Saponis,   1½ gr. }
	50	2 25

Sedative......................
Med. prop.—Sedative. Dose, 1 to 2.
  Ext. Sumbul,   ¼ gr. }
  Ext. Valerian,   ¼ gr. }
  Ext. Hyoscyami,   ½ gr. }
  Ext. Cannab. Ind.,   1-10 gr. }
	75	3 50

Silver Nitras. ¼ gr............. Med. prop.—Alterative to Mucous Membrane. Dose, 1 to 4.	75	3 50
Silver Iodid, ¼ gr............. Med. prop.—Alterative to Mucous Membrane. Dose, 1 to 4.	75	3 50

PILLS.	BOTTLE.	
	100	500
Stomachicæ. (Lady Webster.).....	50	2 25
Med. prop.—Stimulating purgative. Dose, 1 to 2.		
Aloe Socot., 2 grs. ⎫		
Gum Mastich., ½ gr. ⎬		
Fol. Rosæ, ½ gr. ⎭		
Strychnina. 1-60 gr. 1-40 gr. 1-32 gr. 1-30 gr. 1-20 gr. 1-16 gr.....	40	1 75
Med. prop.—Nerve stimulant, Tonic. Dose, 1 to 3.		
Strychninæ Sulph. 1-32 gr......	40	1 75
Med. prop.—Nerve stimulant, Tonic. Dose, 1 to 3.		
Syphilitic............	1 00	4 75
Med. prop—Specific alterative. Dose, 1 to 2.		
Potass. Iodid., 2½ grs. ⎫		
Hyd. Chlor. Cor., 1-40 gr. ⎭		
Tonic.........	60	2 75
Med. prop.—Tonic. Dose, 2 to 3.		
Ext. Gentian, 1 gr. ⎫		
Ext. Humuli, ½ gr. ⎪		
Ferri Carb. Sacch., ¼ gr. ⎪		
Ext. Nuc. Vom., 1-20 gr. ⎬		
Res. Podophylli, 1-25 gr. ⎪		
Ol. Res. Zingiber., 1-10 gtt. ⎭		
Triplex...................	75	3 50
Med. prop.—Purgative. Dose, 2 to 4.		
Aloe Socot., 2 grs. ⎫		
Mass. Hydrarg., 1 gr. ⎬		
Podophyllin, ¼ gr. ⎭		
Triplex Improved..............	75	3 50
Med. prop.—Purgative. Dose, 2 to 4.		
Pv. Scammon. Virg., 1 1-5 gr. ⎫		
Pv. Aloes Soct., 1 1-5 gr. ⎪		
Pil. Hydrarg., 1 1-5 gr. ⎬		
Ol. Tiglii, 1-20 ℳ. ⎪		
Ol. Carui, ¼ ℳ. ⎪		
Tinct. Aloes et Myrrh., q. s. ⎭		
Zinc Phosphide. ⅛, ¼ gr........	75	3 50
Med. prop.—Tonic. Dose, 1 to 3.		
Zinci Phosphide et Nuc. Vom.	1 00	4 75
Med. prop.—Tonic, Stimulant. Dose, 1 to 3.		
Zinci Phos., 1-10 gr. ⎫		
Ext. Nuc. Vom., ¼ gr. ⎭		
Zinci Valerianas. 1 gr...........	1 00	4 75
Med. prop.—Anti-spasmodic. Dose, 1 to 3.		

40

WARNER & CO.'S

SOLUBLE COATED

GRANULES.

GRANULES.	BOTTLE.	
	103	500
Acid Arsenious. 1-20, 1-30, 1-50, and 1-60 gr...... Medical properties.—Anti-periodic, Alterative. Dose, 1 to 2.	40	1 75
Aconitin. 1-60 gr............ Med. prop.—Nerve sedative. Dose, 1 to 2.	75	3 50
Aloin et Strychnin............ Med. prop.—Tonic laxative. Dose, 1 to 2.	60	2 75
Aloin et Strychnin. et Belladon.................... Med. prop.—Tonic, Laxative. Dose, 1 to 2. Aloin, 1-5 gr. Strychnine, 1-60 gr. Ext. Belladon., ⅛ gr.	60	2 75
Atropinn. 1-60 gr.............. Med. prop.—Anodyne. Dose, 1 to 2.	75	3 50
Atropina. 1-100 gr.............. Med. prop.—Anodyne. Dose, 1 to 2.	75	3 50
Atropinæ Sulph. 1-60 gr........ Med. prop.—Same as Atropina. Dose, 1 to 2.	75	3 50
Caulophyllin. 1-10 gr........... Med. prop.—Emmenagogue. Dose, 1 to 4.	40	1 75
Cimicifugin. 1-10 gr............ Med. prop.—Tonic, Nerve stimulant. Dose, 1 to 4.	40	1 75
Codein. ¼ gr................... Med. prop.—Anodyne, replacing morphia without the usual disagreeable after-effects produced by the latter. Dose, 2 to 4.	1 25	6 00
Corrosive Sublimate. 1-12, 1-20, 1-40, and 1-100 gr.............. Med. prop.—Mercurial alterative. Dose, 1 to 2.	40	1 75

47

GRANULES.	BOTTLE.	
	100	500
Digitalin. (Alkaloid.) 1-60 gr...... Med. prop.—Arterial sedative. Dose, 1 to 2.	75	3 50
Elaterium. (Clutterbuck's) 1-10 gr. Med. prop. — Diuretic, Hydragogue cathartic. Dose, 1 to 2.	95	4 50
Ext. Belladonna. (English) ¼ gr Med. prop.—Anodyne. Dose, 1 to 3.	40	1 75
Extract Cannabis Indica. ¼ gr. Med. prop.—Anodyne. Dose, 1 to 4.	60	2 75
Extract Hyoscyam. (Eng.) ½ gr. Med. prop.—Nerve stimulant. Dose, 1 to 3.	40	1 75
Extract Ignatia Amara. ¼ gr.. Med. prop.—Nerve sedative. Dose, 1 to 2.	50	2 25
Extract Nuc. Vom. ¼ and ½ gr.. Med. prop.—Nerve stimulant. Dose, 1 to 3.	40	1 75
Gelsemin. 1-16 gr.................... Med. prop.—Arterial sedative. Dose, 1 to 4.	40	1 75
Gelsemin. ⅛ gr.................... Med. prop.—Arterial sedative. Dose, 1 to 2.	50	2 25
Gelsemin. ¼ gr.................... Med. prop.—Arterial sedative. Dose, Dose, 1 to 2.	75	3 50
Helonin. 1-10 gr.................... Med. prop.—Cathartic. Dose, 1 to 4.	50	2 25
Hydrastin. ½ gr.................... Med. prop.—Cathartic. Dose, 1 to 2.	95	4 50
Hyoscyamiæ. 1-100 gr............. (Crystals, Pure Alkaloid.) Med. prop.—Anodyne, Soporific. Dose, 1.	3 00	14 75
Leptandrin. ¼ gr................... Med. prop.—Cathartic. Dose, 1 to 4.	40	1 75
Leptandrin. ½ gr................... Med. prop.—Cathartic. Dose, 1 to 4.	50	2 25
Mercury Bin-Iodide. 1-16 gr.... Med. prop.—Anodyne. Dose, 1 to 4.	40	1 75

GRANULES.	BOTTLE.	
	100	500
Mercury Protiodide. ¼ gr...... Med. prop.—Alterative. Dose, 1 to 4. Prepared from the precipitated Iodide and free of all traces of the Bin-Iodid.	40	1 75
Mercury Protiodide. ½ gr...... Med. prop.—Alterative. Dose, 1 to 2.	50	2 25
Mercury Protiodide. ⅛ gr...... Med. drop.—Alterative. Dose, 2 to 4.	40	1 75
Mercury Protiodide. 1-5gr...... Med. prop.—Alterative. Dose, 1 to 4.	40	1 75
Morphinæ Acet. ⅛ gr........... Med. prop.—Anodyne. Dose, 1 to 2.	70	3 25
Morphinæ Sulph. 1-20 gr........ Med. prop.—Anodyne. Dose, 1 to 2.	40	1 75
Morphinæ Sulph. 1-10 gr........ Med. prop.—Anodyne. Dose, 1 to 2.	50	2 25
Morphinæ Sulph. ⅛ gr.......... Med. prop.—Anodyne. Dose, 1 to 2.	60	2 75
Morphinæ Sulph. ⅙ gr.......... Med. prop.—Anodyne. Dose, 1 to 2.	70	3 25
Morphinæ Sulph. ¼ gr.......... Med. prop.—Anodyne. Dose, 1 to 2.	90	4 25
Morphinæ Sulph. ½ gr.......... Dose, 1.	1 50	7 25
Morphinæ Valer. ⅛ gr.......... Med. prop.—Anodyne. Dose, 1 to 2.	90	4 25
Podophyllin. 1-10 gr............ Med. prop.—Cathartic. Dose, 1 to 4.	40	1 75
Podophyllin. ¼ gr.............. Med. prop.—Cathartic. Dose, 1 to 4.	40	1 75
Podophyllin. ½ gr.............. Med. prop.—Cathartic. Dose, 1 to 2.	50	2 25
Podophyllin Comp............. Med. prop.—Cathartic and Tonic. Dose, 1 to 2. Podophyllin, ½ gr. Ext. Hyoscyami, ⅛ gr. Ext. Nuc. Vom., 1-16 gr.	75	3 50

GRANULES.	BOTTLE.	
	100	500
Silver Iodid. ¼ gr................... Med. prop. — Alterative to Mucous Membrane. Dose, 1 to 4.	75	3 50
Silver Nitrate. ¼ gr............... Med. prop. — Alterative to Mucous Membrane. Dose, 1 to 4.	75	3 50
Strychnin. 1-16, 1-20, 1-30, 1-32, 1-40, and 1-60 gr........................ Med. prop.—Nerve stimulant, Tonic. Dose, 1 to 3.	40	1 75
Strychninæ Sulph. 1-32......... Med. prop.—Tonic. Dose, 1 to 2.	40	1 75
Veratrinæ Sulph. 1-12 gr........ Med. prop.—Powerful topical excitant. Dose, 1.	50	2 25
Zinc Phosphide. ⅛ and ¼ gr.... Med. prop.—Tonic. Dose, 1 to 3.	75	3 50

SOLUBLE COATED

Pills and Granules.

I have used WILLIAM R. WARNER & CO.'S SUGAR-COATED PILLS for more than fifteen years, and I do not hesitate to say that, in respect of solubility, THEY ARE SUPERIOR TO ANY COATED PILLS I HAVE EVER TRIED, not excepting those coated with gelatine. They possess one quality which I do not find in most other pills, viz: a moist condition of the enclosed ingredients.   ROBT. HUBBARD, M. D.

Bridgeport, Conn.

WARNER & CO.'S
PHOSPHORUS PILLS.

A TABLE OF COMBINATIONS.	Bottles 100
1.—Pil. Phosphori. 1-25 gr............	1 00

Medical properties.—Nerve stimulant.
Dose, 1.

The method of preparing Phosphorus in pilular form has been *discovered and brought to perfection by us*, without the necessity of combining it with resin, which forms an insoluble compound. The element is in a perfect state of subdivision and incorporated with the excipient while in solution. The non-porous coating of sugar protects it thoroughly from oxidation, so that the pill is not impaired by age. It is the most pleasant and acceptable form for the administration of Phosphorus.

2.—Pil. Phosphori. 1-50 gr............   1 00
Med. prop.—Nerve stimulant. Dose, 1.

3.—Pil. Phosphori. 1-100 gr.........   1 00
Med. prop.—Nerve stimulant. Dose, 1.

4.—Pil. Phosphori Comp 1 25
Med. prop.—Nerve tonic. Dose, 1.
Phosphori,   1-100 gr. }
Ext. Nuc. Vom.,   ¼ gr. }

5.—Pil. Phosphori cum Nuc. Vom   1 25
Med. prop.—Nerve tonic and Stimulant.
Dose, 1 to 2.
Phosphori,   1-50 gr. }
Ext. Nuc. Vom.,   ⅛ gr. }

6.—Pil. Phosphori cum Ferro....   1 25
Med. prop.—A Powerful Nervine tonic and
Blood restorer. Dose, 1 to 2.
Phosphori,   1-50 gr. }
Ferri Redact.,   1 gr. }

7.—Pil. Phosphori cum Ferro et Nuc. Vom......................   1 25
Med. prop.—Nerve stimulant, Tonic. Dose, 1 to 2.
Phosphori   1-100 gr. }
Ferri Carb.,   1 gr. }
Ext. Nuc. Vom.,   ¼ gr. }

A TABLE OF COMBINATIONS.	Bottles 100
8.—Pil. Phosphori cum Ferro et Quinina.................... Med. prop.—Nerve tonic. Dose, 1 to 2. Phosphori, 1-100 gr. Ferri Carb., 1 gr. Quininæ Sul., 1 gr.	1 60
9.—Pil. Phosphori cum Ferro et Quinina et Nuc. Vom......... Med. prop.—Nerve tonic. Dose, 1 to 2. Phosphori, 1-100 gr. Ferri Carb., 1 gr. Quininæ Sul., 1 gr. Ext. Nuc. Vom., ¼ gr.	1 60
10.—Pil. Phosphori cum Quinina Med. prop.—Nerve tonic. Dose, 1 to 2. Phosphori, 1-50 gr. Quininæ Sul., 1 gr.	1 80
11.—Pil. Phosphori cum Quinina Comp..................... Med. prop.—Nerve tonic. Dose, 1. Phosphori, 1-50 gr. Ferri Redact., 1 gr. Quininæ Sul., ½ gr. Strychnin, 1-60 gr.	1 25
12.—Pil. Phosphori cum Quinina et Nuc. Vom............... Med. prop.—Nerve tonic. Dose, 1 to 2. Phosphori, 1-30 gr. Quininæ Sul., 1 gr. Ext. Nuc. Vom., ¼ gr.	1 60
13.—Pil. Phosphori cum Quinina et Digitale Co............ Med. prop.—Valuable as a Sedative and Diuretic. Dose, 1 to 2. Phosphori, 1-50 gr. Quininæ Sul., ½ gr. Pv. Digitalis, ½ gr. Pv. Opii, ¼ gr. Pv. Ipecac., ¼ gr.	1 35
14.—Pil. Phosphori cum Digitale Comp.................... Med. prop.—Valuable as a Heart tonic. Dose, 1. Phosphori, 1-50 gr. Pv. Digitalis, 1 gr. Ext. Hyoscyami, 1 gr.	1 50

46

A TABLE OF COMBINATIONS.	Bottles 100

15.—Pil. Phosphori cum Digitale et Ferro................. 1 50
Med. prop.—Valuable as a Heart tonic.
Dose, 1.
Phosphori,   1-50 gr.
Pv. Digitalis,   1 gr.
Ferri Redact.,   1 gr.

16.—Pil. Phosphori cum Cannabe Indica................. 1 75
Med. prop.—Narcotic, Aphrodisiac. Dose, 1 to 2.
Phosphori,   1-50 gr.
Ext. Cannab. Ind.,   ¼ gr.

17.—Pil. Phosphori cum Morphina et Zinco Val................. 2 00
Med. prop.—Nerve tonic and Sedative.
Dose, 1.
Phosphori,   1-50 gr.
Morphniæ Sul.,   1-12 gr.
Zinci Valer.,   1 gr.

18.—Pil. Phosphori cum Aloe et Nuce Vomica................. 1 50
Med. prop.—Useful in the Atonic Form of Dyspepsia and Neurosis of the Stomach. Dose, 1.
Phosphori,   1-50 gr.
Ext. Aloes Aq.,   ½ gr.
Ext. Nuc. Vom.,   ¼ gr.

19.—Pil. Phosphori cum Zinco Comp................. 1 50
Med. prop.—Useful in Uterine disturbances, Leucorrhœa, and Hysteria. Dose, 1 to 2.
Phosphori,   1-50 gr.
Zinci Sul.,   1 gr.
Lupulin,   1 gr.

20.—Pil Phosphori cum Opio et Digitale................. 1 50
Med. prop.—Useful in Arresting Abnormal calorifications. Dose, 1 to 2.
Phosphori,   1-50 gr.
Pv. Digitalis,   ½ gr.
Pv. Ipecac.,   ¼ gr.
Pv. Opii,   ¼ gr.

A TABLE OF COMBINATIONS.	Bottles 100
21.—Pil. Phosphori cum Strych.. Med. prop.—Nerve tonic and Stimulant. Dose, 1. Phosphori, 1-50 gr.) Strychnin, 1-60 gr.)	1 25
22.—Pil. Phosphori cum Cantharide Comp Med. prop.—Stimulating emmenagogue and Diuretic. Dose, 1 to 2. Phosphori, 1-50 gr.) Pv. Nuc Vom., 1 gr.) Sol. Canthar. Conct., 1 ⅠⅡ.)	1 50
23.—Pil. Phosphori cum Belladonna Med. prop.—Useful in Anæmic Conditions and Neuralgia. Dose, 1 to 2. Phosphori, 1-100 gr.) Ext. Belladonnæ, ⅛ gr.)	1 50
24.—Pil. Phosphori cum Ferro et Strychnina Med. prop.—Nerve tonic and Stimulant. Dose, 1 to 2. Phosphori, 1-100 gr.) Ferri Carb., 1 gr.) Strychnin, 1-60 gr.)	1 50
25.—Pil. Phoshpori cum Quinina et Ferro et Strychnina Med. prop.—Powerful nerve stimulant. Dose, 1. Phosphori, 1-100 gr.) Quininæ Sul., 1 gr.) Ferri Redact., 1 gr.) Strychnin, 1-60 gr.)	1 60
26.—Pil. Phosphori cum Ext. Aconiti Med. prop.—Useful in the Treatment of Phthisis with Pyrexia. Dose, 1.	1 50
27.—Pil. Phosphori et Damiana cum Nuc. Vom. Med. prop.—Aphrodisiac. Dose, 1 to 2. Phosphori, 1-100 gr.) Ext. Damiana, 2 grs.) Ext. Nuc. Vom., ⅛ gr.)	1 50

48

ADDENDA

SOLUBLE COATED PILLS

PILLS.	BOTTLE.	
	100	500
Enonymin. 2 grs.	2 00	9 75
Med. prop.—Tonic, Laxative, Diuretic. Dose, 1 to 2.		
Cocaine Hydrochlor. 1-10 gr.	1 50	7 25
Med. prop.—Stimulant, Tonic, Aphrod'siac.		
Ergotin. 2 grs.	1 25	6 00
Med. prop.—Parturient. Dose, 1 to 2.		
Ext. Eucalyptus. 2 grs.	1 00	4 75
Med. prop.—Diaphoretic, Febrifuge.		
Morphinæ Murias. ½ gr.	1 50	7 25
Med. prop.—Anodyne, Soporific. Dose, 1.		
Morphinæ Murias. ¼ gr.	90	4 25
Med. prop.—Anodyne, Soporific.		
Morphinæ Murias. ⅛ gr.	60	2 75
Med. prop.—Anodyne, Soporific. Dose, 1 to 2.		
Nickel Bromid. 2½ grs.	1 50	7 25
Med. prop.—Recommended in Epilepsy. Dose, 1 to 2.		
Sumbul Comp.	1 50	7 25
Ext. Sumbul, 1 gr.		
Asafœtida, 2 grs.		
Ferri Sulph. Exsic., 1 gr.		
Acid Arsen., 1-30 gr.		

49

PILLS.	BOTTLE.	
	100	500
Quinina et Ferri et Zinci Valer.	1 50	7 25

Quinina et Ferri et Zinci Valer.
  Med. prop.—Recommended for the relief of Melancholia, Incipient Insanity, and as being particularly adapted for the cure of the worry of nervous females.
    Dose, 1.
    Quininæ Valer.
    Ferri Valer.
    Zinci Valer, āā 1 gr.

Chalybeate Comp. (Warner & Co.) 80
  Med. prop.—Employed in the treatment of Anemia, Chlorosis, Phthisis, etc. Dose, 1 to 3.
    Chalybeate Mass.   2 grs.)
    Ext. Nuc. Vom.   ½ gr.)

Manganese Bin-Oxide. 2 grs... 1 25 6 00
  Med. prop.—Emmenagogue. Dose, 1.

Aloin. ¼ gr.   75 3 50
  Med. prop.—Laxative. Dose, 1 to 3.

Antiseptic. (Warner & Co.) 80
  Med. prop.—Pil. Antiseptic is prescribed with great advantage in cases of Dyspepsia attended with Acid Stomach and Enfeebled Digestion following an over indulgence in eating or drinking. It is also useful in Rheumatism. Dose, 1 to 3.
    Sulphite Soda,   1 gr.)
    Salicylic Acid,   1 gr.)
    Ext. Nuc. Vom.   ¼ gr.)

Antiseptic Comp. (Warner & Co.) 80
  Med. prop.—Used with great advantage in cases of Dyspepsia, Indigestion and Malassimilation of food. Dose, 1 to 3.
    Sulphite Soda,   1 gr.)
    Salicylic Acid,   1 gr.)
    Ext. Nuc. Vom.   ½ gr.)
    Powd. Capsicum,   1-10 gr.)
    Concent. Pepsin,   1 gr.)

Lapacticæ   75 3 50
    Aloin,   ¼ gr.)
    Strychnin,   1-60 gr.)
    Ext. Belladon.   ½ gr.)
    Ipecac,   1-10 gr.)

A NEW
Important Class of Remedies.
PARVULES.

This is a new class of medicines (minute pills), designed for the administration of remedies in small doses for frequent repetition in cases of children and adults. It is claimed by some practitioners that small doses, given at short intervals, exert a more salutary effect. *The elegence and efficiency of Parvules, and the avoidance of cumulative effect, depend on our mode of preparation.*

THE DOSE

of any of the parvules will vary from one to four, according to age or the frequency of their administration. For instance, one Parvule every hour, or two every two hours, or three every three hours, and so on for adults. For children, one three times a day is the minimum dose.

PRICE, 26 CENTS PER BOTTLE OF 100 EACH. DISCOUNT FOR QUANTITIES.

POCKET CASES, WITH 20 VARIETIES, FOR THE USE OF PRACTITIONERS, $5.00 NET.

POCKET CASES, WITH 10 VARIETIES, FOR THE USE OF PRACTITIONERS, $2.50.

HAND OR BUGGY CASES, 40 BOTTLES, ALL THE VARIETIES, $10.00 NET.

SUPPLIED BY ALL DRUGGISTS, OR SENT BY MAIL ON RECEIPT OF PRICE.

Acidi Arseniosi...........................1-100 gr.
    Medical properties.—Alterative, Anti-periodic.

Acidi Salicylic...........................1-10 gr.
    Med. prop.—Anti-rheumatic.

51

Acidi Tannic......................................1-20 gr.
  Med. prop.—Astringent.

Aconiti Rad....................................1-20 gr.
  Med. prop.—Narcotic, Sudorific.

Aloin..1-10 gr.
  Med. prop.—A most desirable cathartic.

Dose.—4 to 6 at once. This number of Parvules, taken at any time, will be found to exert an easy, prompt, and ample cathartic effect, unattended with nausea, and in all respects furnishing the most desirable aperient and cathartic preparation in use. For habitual constipation they replace, when taken in single Parvules, the various medicated waters without the quantity which they require as a dose, which fills the stomach and deranges the digestive organs.

Ammonii Chlorid........................1-10 gr.
  Med. prop.—Diuretic, Stimulant.

Antimonii et Potass. Tart.........1-100 gr.
  Med. prop.—Expectorant, Alterative.

Arnicæ Flor................................1-5 gr.
  Med. prop.—Narcotic, Stimulant, Diaphoretic.

Arsenici Iodid..........................1-100 gr.
  Med. prop.—Alterative.

Belladonnæ Fol........................1-20 gr.
  Med. prop—Narcotic, Diaphoretic, Diuretic.

Calomel......................................1-20 gr.
  Med. prop.—Alterative, Purgative.

Dose.—1 to 2 every hour. Two Parvules of calomel, taken every hour until five or six doses are administered (which will comprise but half a grain), produce an activity of the liver which will be followed by bilious dejections and beneficial effects that twenty grains of blue mass or ten grains of calomel rarely cause, and sickness of the stomach does not usually follow.

Calomel et Ipecac................ āā 1-10 gr.
  Med. prop.—Alterative, Purgative.

Camphoræ................................1-20 gr.
  Med. prop.—Diaphoretic, Carminative.

Cantharidis..............................1-50 gr.
  Med. prop.—Diuretic, Stimulant.

Capsici ....1-20 gr.
   Med. prop.—Stimulant and Carminative.

Cathartic Comp., Officinal ....⅓ gr.
   Med. prop.—Cathartic.

Cathartic Comp., Improved ....⅓ gr.
   Med. prop.—Cathartic.

Digitalis Fol ....1-20 gr.
   Med. prop.—Sedative, Narcotic, Diuretic.

Dover's Powder ....⅓ gr.
   Med. prop.—Anodyne, Soporific.

Ergotin ....1-10 gr.
   Med. prop.—Emmenagogue, Parturient.

Ferri Redact ....1-10 gr.
   Med. prop.—Tonic.

Gelsemini Rad ....1-50 gr.
   Med. prop.—Nervous and Arterial Sedative.

Hydrarg. Bi-Chlor ....1-100 gr.
   Med. prop.—Mercurial alterative, Germicide.

   Recently, Corros. Sub., in small doses, has been administered with most gratifying results in certain forms of Chronic Dyspepsia.

   Dose.—One Parvule, repeated according to the age or nature of the disease. Ringer and other eminent therapeutists extol very highly 1-100 gr. in dysentery of children, regarding it as almost *specific*.

Hydrarg. cum Creta ....1-10 gr.
   Med. prop.—Alterative.

Hydrarg. Iodid ....1-20 gr.
   Med. prop.—Alterative.

Hydrastin ....1-20 gr.
   Med. prop.—Tonic, Astringent.

Iodoform ....1-10 gr.
   Med. prop.—Alterative.

Ipecac ....1-50 gr.
   Med. prop.—Emetic, Expectorant.

Morphinæ Sulph ....1-30 gr.
   Med. prop.—Narcotic, Sedative.

Nucis Vomicæ............................1-50 gr.
    Med. prop.—Tonic, Stimulant.

Opii..1-40 gr.
    Med. prop.—Narcotic, Sedative, Anodyne.

Phosphorus.............................1-200 gr.
    Med. prop.—Nerve stimulant.

Piperin.................................1-20 gr.
    Med. prop.—Tonic, Anti-periodic, Carminative.

Podophyllin.............................1-40 gr.
    Med. prop.—Carhartic, Cholagogue.

Two parvules of podophyllin administered three times a day will re-establish and regulate the peristaltic action and relieve habitual constipation, add tone to the liver, and invigorate the digestive functions.

Potass. Arsenitis................1-100 gr.
    Med. prop.—Alterative.

Potass. Bromid.........................1-5 gr.
    Med. prop.—Alterative, Resolvent.

Potass. Nitratis.......................1-10 gr.
    Med. prop.—Diuretic and Refrigerant.

Quinine Sulphas....................1-10 gr.
    Med. prop.—Tonic, Anti-periodic.

Santonin.............................1-10 gr.
    Med. prop.—Anthelmintic.

Strychninæ............................1-100 gr.
    Med. prop.—Nerve stimulant, Tonic.

PREPARED ONLY BY

WILLIAM R. WARNER & CO.,

1228 MARKET STREET,

PHILADELPHIA.

DOSIMETRIC GRANULES.

WM. R. WARNER & CO.

As their name indicates, these Granules are *measured doses* of the alkaloids, metals and metalloids in such definite and accurate proportions as may best meet the requirements of the physician.

The most perfect system of Dosimetry is that comprised in Parvules originally introduced by Warner & Co. several years ago, but Dosimetric Granules are intended to comprise such remedies as are new and such as are *proximate principles* not so frequently repeated in a measured time for all cases.

These Granules have been divided according to the metric system into strengths of half milligramme, one milligramme and centigramme. In each instance, however, their equivalents are stated in *grains* or fractions thereof. Such a plan, we think will easily familiarize the practitioner with the metric system for all practical purposes and will commend itself at once to his recognition.

The selection of the list is based entirely upon the *physiological action* of these active or essential principles, and are therefore administered upon a rational basis, thus making therapeutics stand upon firmer ground than that which it has occupied or even still occupies, when compared with the advances which its sister sciences have taken within the last decade. Under the administration of these Granules, therapeutics partake of the character of a *specific* form of treatment.

The cutting short or strangulation of many acute diseases, while as yet in their incipient or formative stages has not been sufficiently appreciated. That this is possible, the medical literature of the day affords ample evidence; but to accomplish it, treatment must be both scientific and energetic, i. e., must be based upon the physiological action of drugs and upon the action of reliable medications.

With such an intention, these Granules have been prepared abroad, (in France particularly as suggested by Dr. Burggraeve.)

This method of treatment has met with success, and it will be a matter of no surprise that therapeutists in this country should be prompt in adopting it.

In the hands of the physician and *his hands only*, these Granules are potent remedies, capable of accomplishing results far more quickly and certainly than the uncertain fluid extracts and tinctures, and far more pleasantly.

See following pages for list comprising 56 varieties.

PREPARED BY

WM. R. WARNER & CO.

MANUFACTURING CHEMISTS,

PHILADELPHIA AND NEW YORK.

DOSIMETRIC GRANULES.

The dose is one Granule, repeated to meet the requirements of the case.

Per 100

Aconitin...............1-65 gr. (1 milligram)$ 75
Med. prop.—Nerve sedative.

Acid Arseniosum....1-65 gr. (1 milligram) 40
Med. prop.—Anti-periodic, Alterative.

Acid Phosphoric.....1-65 gr. (1 milligram) 40
Med. prop.—Nerve stimulant.

Acid Tann. Jcum.......¼ gr. (1 centigram) 40
Med. prop.—Astringent.

Acid Salicylicum......⅙ gr. (1 centigram) 40
Med. prop.—Anti-rheumatic.

Antimonii Arsenias..1-65 gr. (1 milligram) 40
Med. prop.—Alterative, Diaphoretic.

Arsenii Iodidum.....1-65 gr. (1 milligram) 40
Med. prop.—Alterative.

Asparagin...........1-65 gr. (1 milligram) 40
Med. prop.—Arterial sedative.

Atropinæ Sulphas.1-130 gr. (½ milligram) 75
Med. prop.—Anodyne, Anti-spasmodic.

Brucin...............1-130 gr. (½ milligram) 40
Med. prop.—Tonic.

Bryonin.............1-65 gr. (1 milligram) 50
Med. prop.—Hydragogue, Cathartic.

Caffeinæ Arsenias....1-65 gr. (1 milligram) 50
Med. prop.—Alterative.

Caffeinæ Citras......1-65 gr. (1 milligram) 50
Med. prop.—Nerve stimulant.

Caffeinæ Valerianas 1-65 gr. (1 milligram) 50
Med. prop.—Stimulant, Anti-spasmodic.

Calabarin. Sulphas.1-130 gr. (½ milligram) 75
Med. prop.—Spinal sedative.

Calomel..............1-65 gr. (1 milligram) 40
Med. prop.—Alterative, Purgative.

Camphoræ Bromated.¼ gr. (1 centigram) 40
Med. prop.—Sedative.

GRANULES ARE NOT PARVULES.

Per 100

Cicutin.................1-130 gr. (½ milligram) 50
Med. prop.—Nerve sedative.

Cicutin. Hydrobromas....1-65 gr.
(1 milligram) 75
Med. prop.—Nerve sedative.

Codein.................1-65 gr. (1 milligram) 75
Med. prop.—Hypnotic sedative.

Colchicin.............1-130 gr. (¼ milligram) 75
Med. prop.—Sedative, Diuretic, Emetic.

Croton Chloral.........⅙ gr. (1 centigram) 75
Med. prop.—Hypnotic.

Cubebin...............1-65 gr. (1 milligram) 50
Med. prop.—Diuretic.

Daturin..............1-130 gr. (½ milligram) 75
Med. prop.—Narcotic, Anodyne.

Diastase................⅙ gr. (1 centigram) 75
Med. prop.—Possesses the power of convert-
ing starch into sugar (of the grape.)

Elaterin..............1-65 gr. (1 milligram) 75
Med. prop.—Purgative.

Emetine...............1-65 gr. (1 milligram) 75
Med. prop—Emetic, Diaphoretic, Expectorant.

Ergotin................⅙ gr. (1 centigram) 40
Med. prop.—Emmenagogue, Parturient.

Ferri Arsenias.......1-65 gr. (1 milligram) 40
Med. prop.—Tonic, Alterative.

Ferri Salicylas........⅙ gr. (1 centigram) 40
Med. prop.—Tonic.

Ferri Valerianas......⅙ gr. (1 centigram) 40
Med. prop.—Tonic, Anti-spasmodic.

Hydrargyri Iodid. Rub..1-65 gr.
(1 milligram) 40
Med. prop.—Alterative.

Hydrargyri Iodid. Vir.⅙ gr. (1 centigram) 40
Med. prop.—Alterative.

Hyoscyamin........1-130 gr. (½ milligram) 3 00
Med. prop.—Hypnotic, Anti-spasmodic.

GRANULES ARE NOT PARVULES.

Per 100

Iodoform.............1-65 gr. (1 milligram) 40
Med. prop.—Alterative.

Jalapin................1-65 gr. (1 milligram) 50
Med. prop.—Hydragogue cathartic.

Koosin................1-65 gr. (1 milligram) 50
Med. prop.—Anthelmintic.

Lithii Carbonas.......⅙ gr. (1 centigram) 50
Med. prop.—Diuretic.

Lithii Benzoas.........⅙ gr. (1 centigram) 75
Med. prop.—Diuretic, Expectorant.

Morphinæ Hydrobromas..1-65 gr.
(1 milligram) 75
Med. prop.—Anodyne.

Morphinæ Iodohydras....1-65 gr.
(1 milligram.) 75
Med. prop.—Anodyne.

Narcein...............1-65 gr. (1 milligram) 75
Med. prop.—Supposed to influence the inferior part of the spinal marrow, diminishing
the sensation and mobility in the inferior
extremities.

Piperina...............1-65 gr. (1 milligram) 40
Med. prop.—Local and general stimulant.

Picrotoxin...........1-130 gr. (1 milligram) 75
Med. prop.—Narcotic.

Pilocarpin...........1-65 gr. (1 milligram) 75
Med. prop.—Sudorific.

Podophyllin...........⅙ gr. (1 centigram) 40
Med. prop.—Cholagogue cathartic.

Potasii Arsenias....1-65 gr. (1 milligram) 40
Med. prop.—Alterative.

Quassin.......... ....1-65 gr. (1 milligram) 50
Med. prop.—Tonic, Febrifuge, Anthelmintic.

Quininæ Arsenias...1-65 gr. (1 milligram) 50
Med. prop.—Tonic, Alterative.

Quininæ Hydrobromas....⅙ gr.
(1 centigram) 75
Med. prop.—Tonic, Anti-spasmodic.

GRANULES ARE NOT PARVULES.

Per 100

Quininæ Hydroferrocyanas
 1-65 gr. (1 milligram) 75
 Med. prop.—Tonic.

Quininæ Salicylas....⅙ gr. (1 centigram) 75
 Med. prop.—Tonic, Stimulant.

Quininæ Sulphas......⅙ gr. (1 centigram) 75
 Med. prop.—Tonic, Anti-periodic.

Quininæ Valerianas..⅙ gr. (1 centigram) 75
 Med. prop.—Tonic, Anti-spasmodic.

Santonin..............⅙ gr. (1 centigram) 40
 Med. prop.—Anthelmintic.

Scillitin..............1-65 gr. (1 milligram) 50
 Med. prop.—Cardiac sedative, Diuretic.

Sodii Benzoas.........⅙ gr. (1 centigram) 40
 Med. prop.—Diaphoretic, Expectorant.

Sodii Salicylas........⅙ gr. (1 centigram) 40
 Med. prop.—Hepatic stimulant.

Strychninæ Arsenias....1-130 gr.
 (½ milligram) 50
 Med. prop.—Tonic, Alterative.

Strychninæ Hypophos...1-130 gr.
 (½ milligram) 50
 Med. prop.—Tonic.

Strychninæ Sulphas....1-130 gr.
 (½ milligram) 40
 Med. prop.—Tonic.

Sulphur Iodidum.....⅙ gr. (1 centigram) 40
 Med. prop.—Alterative.

Veratrina...........1-130 gr. (½ milligram) 40
 Med. prop.—Topical excitant.

Zinci Cyanidum.....1-65 gr. (1 milligram) 40
 Med. prop.—Anti-spasmodic.

Zinci Phosphidum..1-65 gr. (1 milligram) 40
 Med. prop.—Tonic, Stimulant.

Zinci Valerianas......⅙ gr. (1 centigram) 40
 Med. prop.—Anti-spasmodic.

GRANULES ARE NOT PARVULES.

PARVULE CASES FOR PHYSICIANS' USE.

DELIVERED BY POST ON RECEIPT OF PRICE.

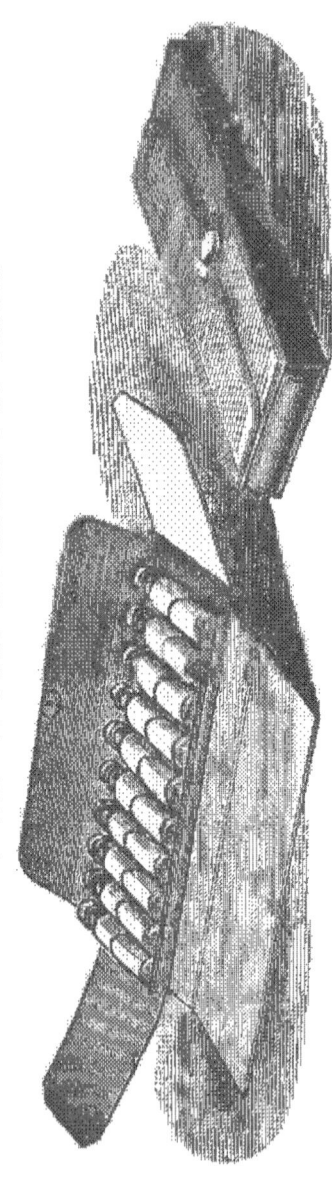

Pocket Parvule Case, filled with ten varieties, any selection, $2.50

This case is of a convenient size for carrying in the coat pocket, and presents a handsome appearance. The dimensions, when closed, are:—Length, 8 in. Width, 3 in. Thickness, 1¼ in.

Manufactured only by WM. R. WARNER & CO.

PARVULE CASES FOR PHYSICIANS' USE.

DELIVERED BY POST ON RECEIPT OF PRICE.

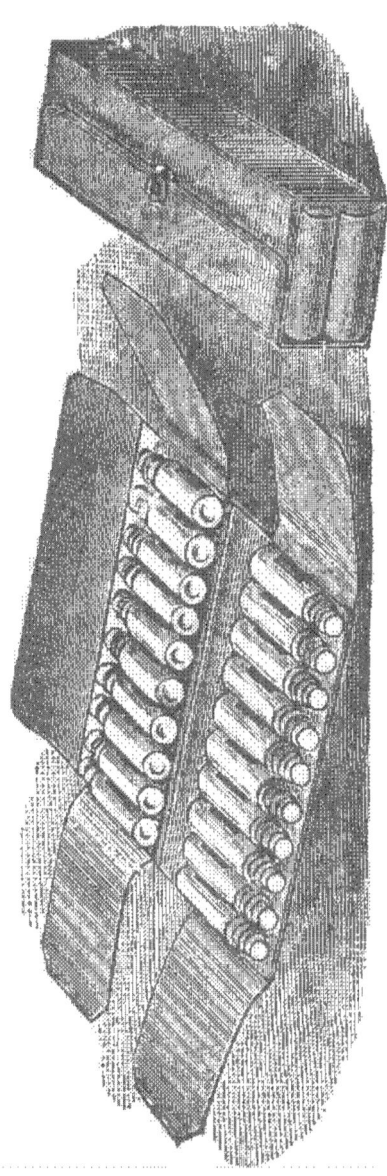

Pocket Parvule Case containing twenty filled bottles, any selection, $5.00

A presentable and compact case suitable for pocket or hand. The dimensions, when closed, are:—Length, 8 in. Width, 3 in. Thickness, 2 in.

Manufactured only by WILLIAM R. WARNER & CO.

PARVULE CASES FOR PHYSICIANS' USE.

DELIVERED BY POST ON RECEIPT OF PRICE.

Warner & Co.'s Buggy or Hand Parvule Case, containing 40 filled bottles, all the varieties, $10.00

Manufactured only by WM. R. WARNER & CO.

Office or Stock Case, glass top, containing forty bottles, full variety, $10.00

DELIVERED FREE ON RECEIPT OF PRICE.

This case with glass top is intended as an office case for Physicians and as a stock or show case for Druggists. It is neat and shows the Parvules to good advantage.

Manufactured only by WM. R. WARNER & CO.

"PARVULES."

Although a practitioner of over forty years, I think I may feel privileged to express my great pleasure and appreciation of the new class of remedies prepared by you called "Parvules." I regard them the greatest improvement in modern medicine, and I could scarcely practice my profession without them, as they are so handy, so convenient, and easily taken by children and adults. Their most important quality is their unvarying and *reliable* strength and efficacy. I can obtain with a grain or less of Calomel, with a grain or less of Aloin, and with a grain or less of Podophyllin, divided respectively into the tenth, twentieth, or fortieth of a grain, in "Parvules," all that I could desire in most cases, and in a more satisfactory manner than in the usual form. I have used successfully a "Parvule" of one-fiftieth of a grain of Sulph. Morphia repeatedly for two or three hours, and have relieved pain without the least nausea or vomiting in patients that could not bear opiates in any other form. I do not know what to attribute this to, except the peculiar mode of preparing the "Parvules," as they are so readily dissolved and absorbed after being taken, and in endorsing them I must disclaim any favoritism or sympathy with Homœopathy. A "Parvule" given every hour, it will be seen, is not Homœopathy in theory or practice. I usually give two "Parvules" of Calomel every hour until six or seven doses are taken, and the result is the same as with ten grains of the same without the embarrassing effect. I give four or five "Parvules" of Aloin, the effect is the same as four or five cathartic pills; also with the Podophyllin "Parvules;" they will relieve habitual constipation, derangement of the liver and digestive organs, if given, one or two, three times a day.

I have no doubt that every practitioner who will use these "Parvules" will find the same results which convinced me of their importance and convenience. I have no other medicine chest in my daily rounds than my pocket case of "Parvules."

Yours very truly,

GEORGE P. REX, M. D.

REAVILLE, N. J.

DOSE TABLE

Showing the ordinary mode of adjusting the dose to suit the age of the patient.

The average adult dose being represented by one, the several doses at different ages may be put down as follows.

Age			Dose
Age	1 to 3 months,	Dose,	1-16
"	4 to 12 "	"	1-10
"	1 to 3 years,	"	$\frac{1}{6}$
"	4 to 5 "	"	$\frac{1}{4}$
"	6 to 8 "	"	$\frac{1}{3}$
"	8 to 12 "	"	$\frac{1}{2}$
"	13 to 16 "	"	$\frac{2}{3}$
"	17 to 20 "	"	$\frac{3}{4}$
"	21 to 45 "	"	1
"	50 "	"	$\frac{3}{4}$
"	60 to 70 "	"	$\frac{2}{3}$
"	80 to 90 "	"	$\frac{1}{2}$
"	100 "	"	$\frac{1}{4}$

The simple rule generally applicable is as follows:

Under 12 years of age diminish the dose of the medicine in the proportion of the age to the age increased by 12 thus:—at 6 years $\frac{6}{6+12}=\frac{1}{3}$.

AN IMPORTANT NEW REMEDY.

SUPERIOR TO PEPSIN OF THE HOG.

A POWDER,

PRESCRIBED IN THE SAME MANNER, DOSES AND COMBINATIONS AS PEPSIN,

INGLUVIN.

VENTRICULUS CALLOSUS GALLINACEUS.

From the Gizzard of the Domestic Fowl, Pullus Gallinaceus.

Dose.—10 to 20 Grains.

A Specific for Vomiting in Pregnancy

AND A

Potent and reliable remedy for the cure of MARASMUS, CHOLERA INFANTUM, INDIGESTION, DYSPEPSIA and SICK STOMACH, caused from debility of that organ. It is superior to the pepsin preparations, since it acts with more certainty, and effects cures where they fail.

PREPARED BY

WM. R. WARNER & CO.

MANUFACTURING CHEMISTS,

PHILADELPHIA and NEW YORK.

SOLD BY DRUGGISTS THROUGHOUT THE COUNTRY, OR SENT BY MAIL TO ANY ADDRESS.

PHYSICIANS WILL PLEASE SEE THAT NO OTHER ARTICLE IS SUBSTITUTED.

68

Abridged Table of Diseases.

For the convenience of Practitioners, we have classified our Pills below, under a heading descriptive of their general properties and the diseases to which they are applicable. The table is necessarily very much condensed. The name of each pill, with formula, will be found on list.

AMENORRHŒA.	Iron, Iodide.
ANÆMIA.	Iron, Cit. and Cinchonidia; Iron, Cit. Quinia; and Phosphorus and Iron.
ASTHMA.	Asafœtida.
BILIOUS FEVER.	Rhubarb Co. and Calomel.
BILIOUSNESS.	Antibilious; Colocy. Ip. and Blue; Cook's; Hepatic; Podophyllin and Podophyllin Compounds generally; Triplex.
BRAIN DISEASES.	Phosphorus, Zinc, Phosphide; Zinc, Phos'ide & Nux.
CATARRH.	Asaf. Comp.
CHLOROSIS.	Iron, (Chalybeate.) Iron, Iodide; Iron, Protocarb; Phosphorus and Iron.
CHOREA.	Cerium, Oxalate.
CONSTIPATION.	See Cathartic and Laxative, in list of Medical Properties.
CONVULSIONS, INF.	Camphor, Monobromated.
CUTANEOUS AFF'NS.	Calcium Sul; Corros. Sub.; Iodoform; Phos. and Iron.
DEBILITY.	Aloes and Myrrh; Iron by Hydrogen; Lupulin; Phosphorus; Phos. Compounds; Phos. I. Q. and Strych.
DELIRIUM TREMENS.	Cannabis Indica.
DIABETES.	Calcium, Sulphide.
DIARRHŒA.	Bismuth, Subnit; Opium; Opium and Camphor.
DROPSY.	Elaterium.
DYSENTERY.	Bis. Subnit.
DYSMENORRHŒA.	Phosphorus, Zinc and Lupulin.
DYSPEPSIA.	Anti-Dyspeptic; Iron by Hydr.; Digestiva; Quinia and Iron Carb.
ERPUTIONS.	Calcium, Sulphide; Calomel Comp.; Corros. Sub.
ERYSIPELAS.	Gelsemin.
FLATULENCE.	Digestiva.

ABRIDGED TABLE OF DISEASES.

GLEET.	Asafœtida Comp.
GONORRHŒA.	Copaiba; Copaiba and Cubebs; Gonorrhœa.
GOUT.	Cannabis Indica.
HEADACHE.	Caffeia, Citrate; Camphor, Monobromated; Guarana Ext.
HOOPING COUGH.	Asafœtida; Belladonna.
HYPOCHONDRIA.	Phos. Nux and Aloes; Phos. Iron and Aloes.
HYSTERIA.	Camphor, Monobrom.; Cannab. Indic.; Iron, Valer.
INDIGESTION.	Leptandrin; Digestiva.
INTERMIT. FEVER.	Cinchonia; Cinchonidia; Gelseminum; Sulph. and Bi-Sulph.; Quinia; Quinidia.
JAUNDICE.	Cathartic Co.; Ox-Gall.
LEUCORRHŒA.	Iron, Iodide; Phos. Zinc and Lupulin.
MELANCHOLIA, FEM.	Phosphorus, Zinc & Lup'n.
NEURALGIA.	Cannab. Indic. Ext.; Neuralgia, Dr. Gross' and Brown-Sequard's; Quinine.
NYMPHOMANIA.	Camphor, Monobromated.
PALSY.	Nux Vomica.
PHTHISIS.	Hypophos. Comp.; Iodoform; Iodoform and Iron; Phosphorous and Ex. Aconite; Phos. Morph. and Valer. Zinc.
PYROSIS.	Cerium, Oxalate.
RHEUMATISM.	Calomel Co.; Cannab. Ind.; Cor. Sub.; Salicylic Acid.
SCIATICA.	Phosphorous and Iron.
SCROFULA.	Calcium, Sulphide; Iodoform; Iodoform and Iron; Mercury, Bin. and Prot. Iodides.
SKIN DISEASES.	Calcium Sulphide.
SPERMATORRHŒA.	Camphor, Monobrom.
SYPHILIS.	Calomel Comp.; Cor. Sub.; Iodoform; Iodof. and Iron; Iron, Iodide; Mercury, Bin. and Proto Iodides; Phosphorous, Q. I. and Strych.
TETANUS.	Cannab. Indica.
TYPHOID FEVER.	Gelseminum; Lupulin.
VOMITING IN PREG.	Cerium Oxalate.

WARNER'S
PIL: CHALYBEATE COMP:

COMPOSITION OF EACH PILL.

℞ (Chalybeate Mass.) Carb. Protoxide of Iron, gr. iiss.
Extract Nux Vomica, gr. ⅙.

Dose.—One or two pills may be prescribed three times a day. They should be taken immediately after eating.

It is truly stated by eminent practitioners that these pills will cause the pale lips to become red and the rosy flush of health to creep into the face in about two weeks' time.

La Progress Medicale; —"Iron is one of the most important principles of the organism and the only metal the presence of which is indispensable to the maintenance of life. It exists in all parts of the system, but nowhere does it acquire such importance as in the blood.

The blood of a person in good condition contains about forty-five grains of Iron; when this amount is diminished a decline takes place, the appetite fails, the strength is enfeebled, and the blood loses its fine natural color and qualities.

In a great number of diseases such as anæmia, chlorosis, hemorrhages, debility, etc., it sometimes happens that the blood has lost half its iron, and, to cure these diseases, it is absolutely necessary to restore to the blood the iron which it lacks, and great care should be exercised that the most assimilable form of iron should be used, one that penetrates into the organism without unduly taxing the digestive tract or interfering with the essential qualities of the gastric juice."

In chloro-anæmia, Warner's Pil. Chalybeate Comp. regenerates the diseased red globules of the blood with a rapidity not before observed under the use of other ferruginous preparations; it adds to their physiological power, and makes them richer in coloring matter. Moreover, being neither styptic nor caustic, and having no coagulating or astringent action on the gastro-intestinal mucous membrane, this preparation of iron causes neither constipation or diarrhœa as it does not need to be digested in order to be absorbed, it does not give rise to the sensation of weight in the stomach, or the gastric pain and indigestion occasioned by other preparations. In women who have not menstruated for many months, the amenorrhœa disappears; in others suffering from an anæmic state of long duration, give in proportion as the ordinary preparations of iron have not been well borne, Warner's Pil. Chalybeate Comp. one or two after each meal, soon restore the digestive functions to their normal state.

The small quantity of Nux Vomica is added to increase the tonic effect, to give tone to the stomach and nerves and increase the appetite.

PREPARED BY

WM. R. WARNER & CO.

PHILADELPHIA AND NEW YORK.

73

TABLE FOR CONVERTING
APOTHECARIES' WEIGHTS and MEASURES
INTO METRIC WEIGHTS.

TROY WEIGHT. (GRAINS.)	GRAMMES.	APOTHECARIES' MEASURES. (MINIMS.)	GRAMMES FOR LIQUIDS.		
			Lighter than water.	Spec. Grav. of water.	Heavier than water.
1-16	.004	1	.055	.06	0.8
1-12	.005	2	.10	.12	.15
1-10	.006	3	.16	.18	.24
⅙	.008	4	.22	.24	.32
⅛	.010	5	.28	.3	.40
¼	.016	6	.32	.36	.48
⅓	.02	7	.38	.42	.55
½	.03	8	.45	.5	.65
¾	.05	9	.50	.55	.73
1	.065	10	.55	.6	.80
2	.13	12	.65	.72	.96
3	.20	14	.76	.85	1.12
4	.26	15	.80	.9	1.20
5	.32	16	.90	1.0	1.32
6	.39	20	1.12	1.25	1.60
7	.45	25	1.40	1.55	2.00
8	.52	30	1.70	1.90	2.50
9	.59	35	2.00	2.20	2.90
10 (℈ ss)	.65	40	2.25	2.50	3.30
12	.78	48	2.70	3.0	4.00
14	.90	50	2.80	3.12	4.15
15	1.00	60 (fƷ i)	3.40	3.75	5.00
16	1.05	65	3.60	4.0	5.30
18	1.18	72	4.05	4.5	6.00
20 (℈ i)	1.3	80	4.50	5.0	6.65
24	1.5	90 (fƷ iss)	5.10	5.6	7.50
30 (Ʒ ss)	1.95	96	5.40	6.0	8.00
32	2.1	100	5.60	6.25	8.30
36	2.3	120 (fƷ ii)	6.75	7.5	10.00
40 (℈ ii)	2.6	150 (fƷ iiss)	8.50	9.5	12.50
45	3.0	160	9.00	10.0	13.30
50 (℈ iiss)	3.2	180 (fƷ iii)	10.10	11.25	15.00
60 (Ʒ i)	3.9	210 (fƷ iiiss)	11.80	13.0	17.50

WARNER & CO.'S

COCAINE POCKET CASE.

Price, $1.75.

This article is put up for use of Surgeons and Dentists, in morocco cases containing two vials of the solution with pipette for dropping, also camels hair pencil, sponge probang, watch glass, etc. The probang is for application in acute nasal Catarrh or Hay Fever.

POISONS AND ANTIDOTES.

COMPILED FROM VARIOUS SOURCES.

☞ In all cases use the stomach pump at once if possible.

INORGANIC POISONS.

ACIDS.

Acetic.
Citric.
Muriatic.
Sulphuric.

Carbonates of sodium, potassium, calcium and magnesium are all antidotes. In the case of sulphuric acid, water should not be drunk, as the union of the two produces great heat. Subsequent inflammation may be treated in the ordinary manner.

Nitric.
Oxalic.

Carbonates of calcium and magnesium alone should be employed; see above.

Prussic.
Laurel Water.
Nitrobenzole.
Oil Bitter Almond.

Ammonia is an antidote but it should not be employed in a very concentrated form. Liquid chlorine has also been found efficacious. The cold *douche* to the head has been recommended.

ANTIMONY.

Butter Antim.
Oxide Antim.
Tarter Emetic.

Vomiting should be produced by tickling the fauces and giving large draughts of warm water. Astringent infusions as galls, oak bark, peruvian bark, act as antidotes, and should be given at once. Powdered yellow bark may be given until the infusion is prepared.

ARSENIC.

White Arsenic

Arsenic Acid.

Yellow Arsen.

Emer'd Green.

Hydrated peroxide iron, diffused through water, or the precipitated carbonate in very fine powder, should be given every five or ten minutes until relief is obtained. This is particularly efficacious where white arsenic has been swallowed.

Dialysed iron solution has come much into vogue at the present time and been highly recommended as an antidote, but the recent experiments of E. Hirschsohn, Russia, prove that when used alone, it has no value whatever in this respect, and, when used in connection with ammonia, or magnesia, the resulting insoluble compound formed with the arsenic, is decomposed much more readily in the presence of acids than when the hydrated peroxide of iron is employed.

COPPER.

and Salts.
Verdigris.
Pickles.

Albumen in form most readily obtained, as milk, white of eggs, &c. Vinegar should *not* be given. The inflammatory and nervous symptoms to be treated on general principles.

LEAD.

Acetate and Carb. Litharge Goulard's Ex.

Sulphate magnesium and phosphate sodium are both good antidotes for the soluble salts. For the solid forms, giving dilute sulphuric acid. The use of strychnia for the paralysis, and of iodide potassium, for the *chronic* forms generally, have been recommended.

MERCURY.

White and Red Precipitate. Cor. Sublimate Vermilion.

Albumen such as white of eggs, milk and wheat flour beaten with water, must be promptly administered. Counteract inflammation by ordinary means. Gold finely mixed in dust with iron filings. The iron filings and *ferri pulvis* have been given enclosed in gold leaf.

ZINC.

Acetate and Sulphate. White Vitriol.

The vomiting may be relieved by copious draughts of warm water. Carbonate sodium in solution will decompose the sulphate. Milk and albumen act as antidotes. General principles to be observed in the subsequent treatment.

CREASOTE.

Is immediately coagulated by albumen.

Phosphorus.

Matches, &c.

An emetic promptly; give copious draughts containing magnesia in suspension; mucilaginous drinks; general treatment for inflammatory symptoms.

ACRONARCOTIC AND NARCOTIC.

Aconite.
Baneberry.
Belladonna.
Bloodroot.
Calabar bean.
Camphor.
Cherry Laurel.
Coce. Indc.
Colchicum.
Curare.
Dogsbane.
Ergot.
Fox Glove.
Gelsemium.
Helebore.
Hemlock.
Henbane.
Lobelia.
Nux Vomica.
Opium.
Poison Oak.
Rue.
Squill.
Strammon.
Tobacco.
Verat. Vir.
Wild Cherry.
Wild Orange.

Evacuate the stomach with four or five grains of tarter emetic, or ten to twenty of sulphate zinc, repeated every quarter hour until the full effect is produced, assist by tickling the throat with a feather. Large and strong glysters of soap dissolved in water, or of salt and gruel, should be speedily administered to clear the bowels and assist in getting rid of the poison. Active purgatives may be given after vomiting has ceased. When as much as possible of the poison has been expelled, give alternately, a teacupful of strong hot coffee and diluted vinegar. If the drowsiness or insensibility be not relieved by these means, blood may be taken from the jugular vein, blisters applied to the neck and legs and the attention roused by every means possible. If the heat declines, warmth and frictions must be perservingly used. Vegetable acid should on no account be given *before* the poison is expelled, and it is desirable that but little fluids of any kind should be administered.

LIQUID

PANCREOPEPSINE

—OR—

LIQUOR PANCREATICUS COMP.

(DIGESTIVE FLUID.)

This preparation contains in an agreeable form the natural and assimilative principles of the digestive fluid of the stomach, comprising **Pancreatine, Pepsin, Lactic and Muriatic Acids.** The best means of re-establishing digestion in enfeebled stomachs, where the power to assimilate and digest food is impaired, is to administer principles capable of communicating the elements necessary to convert food into nutriment.

The value of **Liquor Pancreopepsine** in this connection has been fully established, and we can recommend it with confidence to the profession as superior to pepsin alone. It aids in digesting animal and vegetable cooked food, fatty and amylaceous substances, and may be employed in all cases where from prolonged sickness or other causes, the alimentary processes are not in their normal condition.

It is usually given in tablespoonful doses after each meal, with an equal quantity of water or wine, or alone, as it is most pleasant and agreeable to the taste.

Put up in 16 oz. French Square Bottles

Price, $1.00.

PREPARED ONLY BY

WM. R. WARNER & CO.

PHILADELPHIA AND NEW YORK.

78

ELIXIR

SALICYLIC ACID COMP.

A POTENT AND RELIABLE REMEDY IN

RHEUMATISM, GOUT, LUMBAGO AND KINDRED COMPLAINTS.

This preparation combines, in a pleasant and agreeable form, Salicylic Acid, Cimicifugæ, Gelseminum, Sodii Bi-Carb. and Potass. Iodid., so combined as to be more prompt and effective in the treatment of this class of diseases than either of the ingredients when administered alone.

This remedy can be given without producing any of the unpleasant results which so often follow the giving of Salicylic Acid and Salicylate Sodium—viz., gastric and intestinal irritation, nausea, delirium, deafness, nervous irritability, restlessness and rapid respiration; on the contrary, it gives prompt relief from pain and quiets the nerves without the aid of opiates.

The dose is from a tea to a dessertspoonful. Each teaspoonful contains five grains Salicylic Acid.

Elixir Salicylic Acid Comp. is put up in 12 oz. square bottles.

PREPARED BY

WILLIAM R. WARNER & CO.

MANUFACTURING CHEMISTS,

PHILADELPHIA and NEW YORK.

Special and Private Recipes.

We solicit orders for your Special Recipe, and beg to say that our facilities for the manufacture of

SOLUBLE COATED PILLS,

aided by extensive and improved machinery, enable us to furnish them at moderate prices. We are prepared to fill orders for millions of pills, but we cannot make less quantities than **3000,** it being impracticable to sugar-coat a smaller number.

With a view to their proper manipulation, it is desirable to know the composition. We will therefore supply the ingredients and give the lowest estimate for same. When desired, this may comprise boxes, printing, packing, etc., etc., ready for sale. Our long experience and the favor with which our products are received, attest the excellence of our work.

Soliciting your orders, we are,

Yours respectfully,

WM. R. WARNER & CO.

TEN
WORLD'S FAIR MEDALS
THE HIGHEST FOR THE CLASS
HAVE BEEN AWARDED TO
WM. R. WARNER & CO.
FOR SUPERIORITY OF THEIR
SOLUBLE COATED PILLS
—AND—
GRANULES.

HIGHEST AWARD AT

Vienna, 1873.   Chili, 1875.

Centennial, 1876.   Sydney, 1877.

Paris, 1878.

Sydney, 1879.
Special language on certificate indicating an award
above all competitors.

Melbourne, 1880.
SILVER MEDAL.

Adelaide, 1881.
Gold Medal, the highest award ever given for Pills
of any description.

London, 1881.
Award of Merit, the highest given for Pills.

New Orleans, 1885, Gold Medal.

Language of Award:—"Wm. R. Warner & Co.'s
Soluble Sugar-Coated Pills, first premium for great
uniformity and solubility."

Vermeil Medal, Paris, 1885.

ALSO TWENTY HIGHEST MEDALS AND PREMIUMS
FROM OTHER SOURCES.

www.ingramcontent.com/pod-product-compliance
Lightning Source LLC
Chambersburg PA
CBHW022009050726
47499CB00008BA/2725